TALES OF ELHAANAI

Book Three

WAGES OF WAR

Nicole Patrice Thomas

Cover design by Hannah Sternjakob

Printed in the United States of America
First Printing, 2021
ISBN 978-1-7349192-6-4 (paperback)
978-1-7349192-7-1 (ebook)

This is a work of fiction. Names, characters, businesses, places,
events and incidents either are the products of the author's
imagination or used in a fictitious manner. Any resemblance to
actual persons, living or dead, or actual events is purely coincidental.

INDEX

Dedication

To the ones who would rather read than socialize

Whose eyes worlds can visualize

the ones whose creativity is ostracized

Write the story you've only hypothesized

ELHAANAI

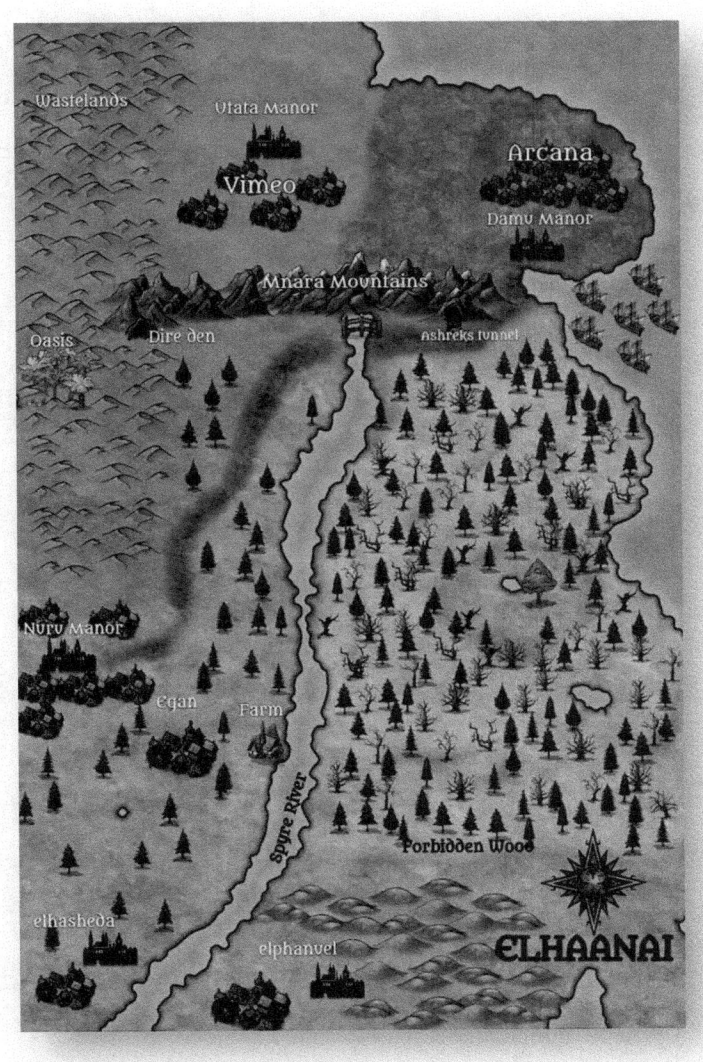

Chapter 1

'When the dead King returns, darkness will follow. Evil will fill places left hollow. One throne, one life, one death to claim, one to alter, one to change. The One to judge the two between, no pawn, no rook, no bishop nor king.'

ALRIC LOOKED AROUND AND WONDERED how long it would take for them to come to the same conclusion he had. As their eyes met, Alric saw understanding appear on Akronius' face.

Akronius turned towards Elainea. "That only leaves... the Queen." His voice was hushed and tinged with awe. All eyes turned to Elainea, whose tanned skin had morphed to ashy gray.

"You can't be serious!" She looked around seeing the doubt and questions swirling across the faces of the others. "You don't believe him right?"

It had been no secret everyone had doubted Alric's strength to be King, but surely they would not back him on this? It was madness. Yet not one person spoke. She took a step back from the group shaking her head. "We have trained and practiced and people have DIED for you to be King. Our MOTHERS DIED believing you to be King, Alric!" She gazed deep into her brother's gray eyes, pleading for him to recant. Instead she saw something she'd never seen before and could not name. "I know you are afraid, but I will not allow you to hide behind that fear. You are meant to be King. I am not. I will NOT be Queen." Turning on her heels, Elainea fled from the group. Away from her home, away from the pressure propelling her towards an unwanted future, and headed towards the solitude of the forest.

Kaison started to go after her, but Alric stopped him with a firm hand on his arm. "Let her go. She will understand in time. There is more I need to tell you that she will not be prepared to hear right now." Casting one last worried glance towards the forest, Kaison nodded and followed Alric as he sat by the fire. One by one the others in the group did the same.

"Will you tell us what happened to you in the forbidden wood?" Keuri asked.

"No, I'm sorry. That journey was meant only for me." Alric smiled, holding the small woman's gaze. "But what I learned is for all of us. The end of the prophecy is clear, as I have told you. And I do believe it means Elainea is meant to be Queen. It was no secret that you all tried to force yourselves to see me as King." Alric's words were spoken lightly, so as not to offend anyone. His father looked guilty, and Akronius couldn't bring himself to meet his eye. "It's alright. I'm meant to do great things, but being King is not one of them. I will return to Shama once the war is over, and take his place on the mountain."

"What? What do you mean?" Kaison said in shock. "You may have the gift of sight, but you are no oracle! How can you... why would you... no! You must be mistaken."

"Father, I know this will be hard to accept. I didn't understand it at first either, but in time it began to make sense. Being an oracle is not necessary to be the guardian of the pool, only the ability to commune with The One. I can, I have and I will continue to do so until He says my work is done."

The fire crackled and a log split sending sparks flying as each person contemplated his words. "I'll admit, I did not hide my doubt in you when we first met," Keuri said, raising her green eyes from the dancing flames to meet his. "But we also believe David is not meant to be on the throne, you would only have been an improvement, albeit a weak one. With your father's and Akronius' guidance, you would have made a fine King. But I will not fight you on this, none of us will." She gestured to her companions, who nodded in agreement.

"Thank you, Keuri." Alric smiled. "I apologize for holding you as I did on our first meeting. You're a strong woman and a strong ally. Elainea will need women, people like you, around her." Keuri lowered the brow at his slip of the tongue before smirking and dipping her head in acknowledgment. "Father, Akronius, this is the way it must be. The One has confirmed it to me and I need you to trust me as I trust Him."

"Alric," Kaison scrubbed his hand over his face, gathering his thoughts. "Son, I know you think this is what must be, but how can it? She is not of noble birth. For the majority of her life she only took care of you, she has no experience or training with being in control and making decisions for so many people. She is part of your family and this group, but no one outside of this home even knows who she is. There has never been a Queen on the throne of Elhaanai. I am sorry. I must disagree with you on this."

"I agree with him, Alric." Akronius said solemnly. "Elainea has grown into a strong woman, but she is no queen. I'm sorry, this makes no sense."

Looking at both men Alric smiled. "And who am I? I have had no ruling experience or training. If not for you being alive, no one would be able to say if I were of noble birth or not because I was NOT of noble birth. To any who know me, Wleia was my mother. Our mother. I know it is hard to believe, but you will see in time."

Silence settled over the group as Alric's words sank in, the truth in them undeniable. The flames crackled and smoke wafted into the sky, floating to the heavens along with the doubts and questions on everyone's mind.

Elainea paced back and forth just beyond the tree line. She felt the wolves watching from the shadows, guarding but distant. The surrounding air rippled from the heat radiating off her skin. Anxiety forced her to release partial control of her gift. *They are wrong. There is absolutely no WAY this is the path my life is meant to take. Alric is King, he will be King.* Thoughts twisted and swirled in her mind, while her breathing became more and more erratic. She could feel pressure rising as angry tears tracked down her face. Her shoulders and chest heaved with each breath. She felt betrayed for some reason, misled and lied to. She was supposed to see Alric to the throne and then go on with her life, marriage to a good man, children, her own home. She had never voiced those desires, but believed they would all come true in time. All of that had potentially been stripped away from her with a few words from Alric. No! She had given up the past few years for him, she didn't resent him for it, but she would not also relinquish her future to rule an entire kingdom.

The fire burned and pulsed just beneath the surface of her skin, causing her whole body to glow slightly red. She had never been this out of control before, she needed a release and quickly. Walking further into the forest, and parallel to the river, she came into a small outcropping of boulders. Planting her feet firmly and facing the largest of the rocks she raised her hands and almost threw the fire out. A steady stream of flames emerged from her palms and surrounded the boulders like a raging river, but it wasn't enough. Tears created a fine haze around her face, evaporating before they could fall far from her eyes. Thoughts of a life she would not have, the continued responsibility she would continue to have to shoulder, the potential addition of a kingdom, all these thoughts brought her to her knees. She had always been the stable one, mature and calm, but not now. Now she screamed and opened every part of herself to the fire, she did not care about the trees around her or the stones or any animals caught in her blaze, for the first time she only cared about herself and the release, the letting go.

She had no idea how long she lay on the scorched earth, but when she opened her eyes the sky was turning shades of pale pink. She sat on the riverbank and watched the sun rise over the horizon. Its rays warming the chill that had settled over her skin. With a deep breath she rose to her feet and caught sight of something twinkling. Glancing back she sucked in a breath, all around her the stones had been turned into crystals. From the smallest pebble to the large boulders, each twinkled and reflected the sunlight in a brilliant display of varying shades. From the ashes of her despair, beauty had been born. Perhaps The One could do the same for her life. Picking one multicolored stone to keep as a reminder, she headed for home.

The sun cast its first rays across Alric's stoic face as he remained by the cooling embers of the fire, watching and waiting for his sister. A wave of heat had brushed the smallest hairs on his neck a few hours ago, and he'd known she was wrestling through her own crucible experience. She was so much stronger than she knew, stronger than any of them could imagine. It would take all of them to bring that strength to the surface, she would just have to trust The One in this new path; they all would. His shoulders lowered in relief as he watched her round the bend in the distance.

"Thank you for not following me. I needed to sort through some things."

"I understand Laney, it's a lot to take in. I was shocked when I found out the rest of prophecy." He paused, then added, "but I was also relieved. You know I..."

"Yes, I know Alric. You had your doubts, we ALL had our doubts. Even more now." She sighed, glancing towards the small band who lay sleeping around the dying embers. "Are you sure Alric? Did you have a vision? Did The One tell you himself that this was the way things are meant to go? Because I will fall in line if that is the case, but I need to be just as sure as you seem to be."

She held Alric's gaze. He did not look away or back down. She could see confidence reflected there.

"Alright then. We need to wake the others and talk this through." Elainea headed inside the small home to make a meal to break their fast. She watched silently as Alric relit the fire with a wave of his hand and began nudging their companions awake. *He really has changed.*

"Father, Akronius, she's back. We need to discuss a plan."

Slowly the group roused themselves, Keuri and her men being the last to wipe the sleep from their heavy lids.

"How is she?" Kaison asked quietly.

"She is uncertain, but open to the change. She's in the house preparing a meal for us."

"I'll go see if she needs any help." Keuri offered, joints popping as she stretched and headed inside the small house. Slamming of cabinetry and plates upon hard surfaces greeted her, along with Elainea's stiff back.

"Looks like it'll snow today." Keuri remarked with deadpan aplomb.

Her red braid whipped around as Elainea turned to meet the smirking face of the only woman she called friend. "Jest all you want. This is crazy and you know it." Elainea placed a wooden pitcher of water on the table with measured concentration, her shoulders lowering in defeat.

"No, I know no such thing. Unconventional? Yes. Uncertain and difficult? Definitely. Crazy? Not at all." Keuri flipped a chair around and sat with her arms resting on its back. "Listen, we all had our doubts about Alric being king, we were quite vocal about that fact, if you recall. He is not a natural born leader. He would have shouldered that mantle if we required it of him, but his own fears and doubts would have undermined and destroyed everyone in the end. YOU on the other hand, have been able to fully develop your strengths and hone your skills, because you did not have that burden of future responsibility weighing you down. You had no desire for the throne."

"Still don't," Elainea interjected.

"I know that," Keuri smiled. "And for that reason, you are perfect. You're strong, you love fiercely and you're loyal. Your temper flares just as quickly as your flames do, but you do not hold grudges for long. If you lack anything, maybe it is the womanly charms of a queen. But that can be easily learned. Trust me, you can do this."

Keuri locked eyes with the young woman before her, she was no whimpering female and seeing her so unsure was unsettling. Just then a breeze parted the overcast sky and a ray of sunlight broke through the clouds landing on a small gem sitting on the windowsill. Its refracted light catching the eye of both woman and causing the beginning of a smile to grace Elainea's face and with it confidence slowly came back into her eyes. Her shoulders set themselves from the concave position they had been in.

"Alright, I'm still not fully on board with this, but we will see it through. Maybe we'll encounter another woman who will better fit this role, but if not and it is truly TRULY the will of The One..." Elainea took a deep breath and then exhaled. "Then I will lead the people back to the light. I will be their Queen."

14

High in the Mnara Mountains, Shama felt the same breeze that brought sunshine onto Elainea's face, and it was as if something clicked into place within him. Breaking the meditative pose he had been sitting in all night, he stood and rushed into his humble home. There against the back wall hidden deep in shadows was an object wrapped in an oil cloth. How could he have forgotten for all this time? His trembling hands grasped the object that was as tall as him, gently unwrapping and letting the covering fall to the floor. It fluttered away like the film that had covered his memory for so long. His staff. It fit into the aged grooves of his hand like an old friend. With determined footsteps he headed back into the yard, blinking rapidly until his eyes adjusted to the sun's glare and the symbols on the staff came into focus as well. Burned into the dark wood, unaffected by time and imbued with the power of the light.

Standing straight he turned to face the eastern sky, bowing from the waist in respect. CRACK! He hit the ground one time with the end of the staff, then brought it horizontal above his shoulder holding it with two hands level with his ear, as if he were about to strike an adversary. Swinging it in a full circle above his head, he pivoted on the balls of his feet until he faced the opposite direction and lunged forward. The moves came back to him with ease and with each simulated attack the words of the staff etched themselves once again across his soul. TRUTH! RIGHTEOUSNESS! FAITH! PEACE! SALVATION! LIGHT! Over and over he went through the poses, the staff moving so rapidly it became a blur. The wind whistled through the twisted stems at the top creating an eerie song to accompany the deadly dance.

Exhausted he dropped to one knee, humbled beyond words under the weight of the coming task. The true words of the prophecy dropped like pebbles on the water of his mind, and he saw the ripples that would soon come. Caressing the wooden staff he headed for the pool that he guarded, but seldom used. Now his mind had been cleared, he had to be purified. The time of sacrifices was at hand, so many would be lost, so many had to be saved.

Stepping to the edge of the pool he remembered Akronius, and wondered how the man fared. So much time had passed since that encounter; he prayed he had stayed true to the course. Placing one foot into the water, he was surprised to find it warm instead of the cool embrace he had been accustomed to. Walking further in he found the temperature increased rapidly. It burned! Everything in him wanted to turn, retreat from the pain. *Refined. Purified.* A voice whispered, brushing across his mind like feathers, so he pressed forward until only his head remained above the water. Again he heard the whisper, *Purified. Refined.* Taking a deep breath he submerged his head, his white locks floating at first before they too followed him beneath the surface.

For a moment he was afraid to open his eyes, the pain blinded him and he forgot where he was. Thrashing around he resisted the urge to inhale; he allowed his fear to overwhelm him. "HELP ME!"

he cried. His last breath escaped in bubbles to the surface, allowing the hot water to rush into his open mouth. When every part of him was completely covered and filled by the liquid and he was sure he could take no more, he inhaled once and then again. Peace settled over him as he floated in the darkness and watched a spark in the distance grow brighter.

"*Shama,*" a voice as loud as thunder sounded from every direction, strong yet gentle, calling his name.

"Yes, my Lord."

"*You have served me well for many years. The prophecy is at hand; will you continue to serve me?*"

"To the end."

"*So be it.*" The voice faded and the heat increased. Shama held his composure as long as he could; he knew the intention was not to cause him pain but to draw all weakness from within him. To refine him into a vessel worthy of the great task he would have to fulfill. Still, it hurt and his humanity screamed until he passed out under the pressure.

When he woke on the bank of the pool, the water was cool once again, and lapped at his ankles. Sitting up he felt no pain, only lightness and freedom. Burdens he must have unconsciously been carrying for years were gone. Picking up the staff from where he had rested it, he headed back down the path. He was the same, but refined with purpose in each step.

Chapter 2

NGUVU KEPT TO THE SHADOWS of the trees as he tracked the one called Chumbra and his female. They argued constantly, and seemed to dislike each other a great deal. He could not understand why they traveled together. They stopped several more times for the pregnant one to relieve herself before finally reaching the village. He would go no further, despite there being very few humans in the streets it would be too dangerous for him. He felt a shift in the atmosphere and the hair along his back rose. Growling, he looked around for the danger but could not find it. Something was very wrong here. Turning, he loped back towards his own pack to report his finding. If he hurried, he would reach them before the sun reached its peak.

"We would have been here hours ago if you could hold your bladder for more than a few moments!" Chumbra complained as they passed through deserted streets heading towards Nuru Manor.

"What makes you think I can't?" Sybella glanced over at the grumbling man beside her. "The few moments in the bushes are a welcome respite from your constant griping."

They both lapsed into silence contemplating their surroundings and what lay before them as the horses brought them further into the village. Each street was void of inhabitants, though she could feel eyes tracking their movement from behind shutters and cracked doors. The silence was oppressive, rotting fruit and human waste littered the street, providing a heavy scent of decay along with a general feel of abandonment. She had always heard such wonderful things about this village that surrounded the great Nuru Manor. The people were light followers, and though naive in their worship, they had prospered. Looking around she could only smirk, *look where it had gotten them. The One cared nothing for his followers. The Dark Lord is the true power. Soon they will all see.*

"Where are all the people?" Sybella asked as they rounded the final bend and entered the courtyard of the manor. The echo of a slamming door reached her ears. The words died on her lips at the sight of the masses before her.

Hundreds of people on bended knees rose to their feet as one, a sea of black capes turned to stare at her with eyes void of emotion. The clip-clop of their horses' hooves was the only sound in the early morning hours. Reaching the steps of the manor, a small boy rushed out and took their reins.

"Welcome back sir," he said, keeping his eyes cast down on the cobblestones at his feet.

"Thank you, Jacob. I trust you have been staying out of trouble in my absence?"

"Yes, sir. I helped in the kitchen and the stables. The head groom said I am a natural."

"I do not care what anyone said about you. Go about your duties." Chumbra's words had extinguished the small spark of pride that had flickered to life in the child's eye. Shoving him to the side, Chumbra hurried inside with Sybella in tow.

Jacob watched the two adults rush into the dark hallways of the manor with hatred brewing behind his hazel eyes. In the short time he had been held captive he had learned to hide his true feelings. Caring for the horses in the stables was the only source of light in what would otherwise be an overwhelmingly dark existence. The sound the brush made against their broad sides brought comfort in its repetitiveness. The whooshing of air from their large noses and the gentle nudges as they sought out secreted pieces of carrot in his threadbare pockets brought a smile to his gaunt face. They were prisoners just as much as he, slaves to a master who neither acknowledged nor cared about their existence, beyond what services they provided him.

Footsteps crunched and scraped against the cobblestone entrance to the stable causing Jacob to wedge himself into a shadowed corner behind a bale of hay. Being small was the same as being invisible, and it afforded him opportunities to listen in on conversations not meant for his young ears.

"Did yer see who that shady oracle drug in wit' him just now?" The burly man said to his companion, another stable hand.

"Aye, I did. It don't bode well for none of us, for the likes of her to be 'ere."

"Nothin' as boded well fer us since... well in long time." The stable master said in a low voice. *That kind of talk would get his head on a spike faster than he could blink if anyone heard him.* Jacob thought from his hiding spot.

"Aye, but ya must'n talk like that, Gerald. You know the penalty if you were to be 'eard."

"Yea, Yea. I know. Still... do ya think what they say is true? Do ya believe em?" Gerald demanded so quietly that Jacob had to strain to hear.

"About, the heir? Yeah. I 'ave a cousin in the south who traveled this way recently. Said they was gathering, welcome anyone willing to join 'em. Brave, but stupid. They don't stand a chance."

"Aye Thomas, stupid indeed. But we can still hope." Gerald said as they made their way back out of the stables.

"Aye, that we can," Thomas concurred with little confidence.

The words lingered in the air as Jacob emerged from the stall he'd been hiding in. He vaguely remembered his parents talking about an heir, though he had no idea who it was. But he did understand people gathering, and if Gerald didn't think they stood a chance that meant they were going to fight the king. And if they were going to fight the king, he wanted to help.

Chapter 3

ASHREK LAY IN THE DARKNESS of his room listening to the wind and rain assault the closed windows. Thunder rattled the panes and lightning streaked across the winter sky, illuminating the emaciated form lying beneath a thin sheet. Ashrek clenched his fists, squeezing his eyes as he concentrated on the few minerals left flowing through his body. Turning his gift inward was the only thing prolonging his life, the curse Sybella had placed on him was working with deadly precision and speed. In the two weeks since she had left with his uncle, his men had searched high and low for someone who could produce a cure or at the very least, a reprieve of the symptoms until the witch could be retrieved and forced to reverse whatever she had done. He found himself regretting the zeal he had taken in rooting out and exterminating followers of the dark magic that plagued him now.

The rap of knuckles against the wooden door filtered through his hazy mind, he grunted an acknowledgment.

"My lord, we have found someone who claims to know how to heal you." The man shifted nervously, averting his eyes from the once strong man barely alive before him.

"Where?" Ashrek whispered, even that small word taxed the miniscule store of strength he had left.

"She is just outside the door sire, shall I show her in?"

"Yes." Ashrek wanted to sit up, to present a strong face, but just breathing was difficult.

The guard stepped outside and motioned for a small girl to enter the room. "Here she is."

"Closer," Ashrek whispered.

The child stepped into the room. Standing near the bed she placed one hand just above Ashrek's chest. "You are close to death, my lord. The curse is flowing freely through your system. You have only hours left to live."

Ashrek squinted his eyes to get a clearer view of the child before him. When another flash of lightning lit up the room, he was surprised to see that she was blind. Not blind in the sense that she could not use her eyes, the place where her eyes should have been was completely smooth and unblemished skin. She had a round face, an earthy complexion framed with ringlets of midnight that cascaded to her waist. She stood in a simple dress, worn through in places with a threadbare shawl clutched around her thin shoulders. Regardless of her attire, she stood as if she were robed with the finest of silks.

"Do not mistake my lack of eyes for a lack of sight. I see with far more clarity and accuracy than you can ever hope to imagine. The girl's head moved as if she were actually looking over his body.

"Explain," Ashrek demanded.

"Where you see flesh and bone, I see spirit or, as in your case, the void caused by a curse and its entry point. You are weak, so I will make this brief. I can cure you. Remove the stain of death that bleeds through your soul. There is a mark between your shoulder and neck, which is the source of the poison. Would you like me to purify you?"

Ashrek was silent as he watched the witchling, she could not have reached her twelfth year and yet she claimed the power to heal him. Nothing came without a cost, and he was hesitant to ask what it would be.

"Cost?" He demanded to know.

"I will require something of you that will aid my sight for a time. You must accept these terms blindly." The child replied calmly.

"Name?" Ashrek inquired.

"Yasmine. Shall we proceed?"

Ashrek hesitated for only a moment. "Yes."

"Turn him." Yasmine instructed the guard, who still stood behind her. "Onto his stomach."

The guard did as she bid, lifting Ashrek who weighed little more than the girl who claimed the power to heal him. Once he was positioned, Yasmine sat on the edge of the bed. "This will hurt."

She did not give Ashrek a chance to respond but placed one hand over the mark and began chanting in a foreign tongue. At first it was just pressure building and building, then the burning started and Ashrek began to scream. The guard slowly backed up, his eyes growing wider as the air in the room became charged with power. Who was this child that she could command such magic! Yasmine turned to face the guard, her skin glowing so brightly it became translucent. *Leave us!* He heard her voice spoken directly into his mind causing him to flee the room, slamming the door behind him as the muffled screams continued.

Bastien stood in the shadows of the Utata Manor, at the end of the corridor whispering rapidly with Rebecca the kitchen maid, when Alcherist approached them.

"What is going on? Everyone in the manor is whispering." Alcherist watched as his two servants cleared their throats and awkwardly avoided his gaze. "Well? One of you had better start explaining."

"Sire, while we are thrilled at the restoration of your son it seems we all may have been tricked in the process." Bastien looked at Rebecca from the corner of his eye, releasing her to scurry away.

"I am waiting." Alcherist had noted the constant whispering and halting of conversation whenever he entered a room. And it had worn his patience to a very thin level.

"Please my Lord, forgive my delay. I am simply relaying what I have learned from those in the village. It is said you simply handed Sybella over to a man no one had previously encountered. And it is believed he was in the employ of King David, so in essence you gave our enemy a very powerful weapon." Bastien whispered the last part, afraid of the repercussion.

"You KNOW that is not the case. There was a mob at the gate demanding her life!" Alcherist dismissed the man with a wave of his hand and continued on his way to his chamber.

"Yes sire, but that is where the confusion lies." Bastien said in a hurry as he walked beside Lord Alcherist. "Once the man and Sybella left the courtyard, the mob simply vanished a short time later. The guards have confirmed it."

Stopping abruptly Alcherist turned. "If the guards confirmed this, a WEEK ago, why has no one brought it to my attention? Why allow that woman to run directly into the safety of an alliance?"

"They were too afraid of your reaction sire! Understandably so, don't you agree? This information is damning for the messenger!" Bastien gulped as Alcherist narrowed his eyes at the one bearing the ill news.

"Yes. It is damning. And a price will be paid. For now, gather my generals. We need a plan of defense should Sybella seek retribution."

"Defense, sir? Don't you mean attack? Surely Ashrek will need…" Bastien said

"Ashrek is a grown man, it is time he handled his own problems. We will not fight someone else's war. Our protection and the protection of our people are our only concern now. See it done." Alcherist shut the door of his chamber in Bastien's face.

Chapter 4

SYBELLA SAT AT THE WORK TABLE watching Chumbra wear a groove in the cobblestone from his constant pacing. He would pick up an object, move it to the other side of the room only to look at it for a moment, shake his head and replace it in its original spot. It was obvious that he was anxious, but for the life of her she couldn't understand why. This man had spent months in the presence of their master; he served him directly and wanted for nothing. If anything, he should be the picture of contentment, having found and fulfilled his master's wish to bring her safely into the fold. Resting her chin in her hand, she leaned on the table. "What is wrong with you Chumbra? Sit down, you're making me nauseous."

"I'm not making you nauseous. It's that spawn you carry that is causing that particular malady. And I pace because it helps me think," Chumbra replied, without breaking his stride. "It calms me."

"Obviously!" Sybella raised one eyebrow. Behind her the door creaked open, and the same child who had taken care of their horses tip-toed in.

"Master, the King has sent for you and the mistress. He waits for you in the dining hall." Jacob said softly.

Sybella watched the child closely. He was thin, underfed and obviously abused, based on the yellowing bruises on his cheek and bare arms. Though she was a follower of darkness, she did not condone mistreatment of slaves. They could be very useful if treated properly.

"What is your name, child?" Sybella walked towards him slowly.

"Jacob, Mistress." He kept his eyes fixed on the floor.

"Look at me, Jacob."

"It is forbidden, mistress." Jacob shifted uncomfortably from foot to foot.

Placing one darkly painted nail beneath his bony chin she lifted his face so she could see him clearly. Still he kept his eyes downcast.

"Do not trouble yourself with the brat, Sybella. The King awaits us. Believe me when I say, we do NOT want to keep him waiting." Chumbra stood in the hall waiting on her.

"Pay him no mind, Jacob. Small men feel the need to speak loudly. Are you hungry? I won't ask if you are cold, the threadbare clothing you are wearing is evident of that fact. Come see me after my meeting, and I will see that you are taken care of. I will need some assistance in this new place and I can tell you are just the one to help me. Agreed?"

For the briefest moment their eyes met. "Agreed, Mistress. I will need to finish cleaning master Chumbra's room first. I will wait here for your return."

"Very well." Sybella smiled brightly at him before exiting the room, following Chumbra down the hall.

As soon as they were out of sight Jacob closed the door and scrubbed the place where she had touched him. Perhaps her softness could be used to his advantage, and if he was fed and provided better clothing in the process, so be it. He hurriedly swept and arranged all the various bowls and cups exactly how Chumbra preferred them, and then he took up his own work. Picking up where he had left off, Jacob skimmed another spell in the book Chumbra had tried to keep hidden. No one suspected that he, a slave, could read. But he hadn't always been a slave. His father had taken pride in his education and made sure its value was instilled deep within him. Though they could not afford formal schooling, he could read, write and cypher as well as most boys who had gone to school. And what he could not understand immediately, he took his time to learn.

He had begun to stockpile small amounts of ingredients for one spell in particular. He had no innate magic that he was aware of, but if spell-casting called for a recipe, he could follow it and hope for the desired outcome. He had read through the spell book several times already, noting which spell had a mark indicating it was successful or not, whether alterations were needed and if it had been used and on whom. There were two that were of special interest to him. One was marked David and the other Devona. He vaguely remembered Devona as the king's mother but having never seen her, he had no idea what she looked like or if she were alive or not. The spell was a very interesting one if it had worked.

Placing the book back into its compartment he wrapped himself in the thin blanket Chumbra had thrown at him one day and sat near the fire to wait for the two evil people to return.

"Your majesty, may I present Lady Sybella." Chumbra bowed deeply, and stepped to the side watching attentively for whatever would happen.

"Sire, I am most pleased that you assisted in my release. How may I return your kindness?" Sybella dipped into a curtsey, and watched the man from beneath her lashes. She could feel the darkness of her master all around her and wondered when he would make his move to reclaim the throne.

I have already reclaimed the throne, daughter. Rise, come closer to me.

Sybella gasped and stood quickly. Darting a glance at a smug Chumbra, she approached the throne. Her eyes narrowed at the obvious fact he had intentionally kept this information to himself.

"Master, I am honored and humbled. How may I serve you?" Sybella stood proudly before the one hosting the spirit of the Dark Lord. Now that she was a few steps away, the darkness in his eyes was evident, as was the power pulsating in waves around him, it was exhilarating.

"You have always served me well, Sybella. However, you are in a unique position at the moment," David said glancing at her belly. "The child within you is not part of my plans. But because of your

31

loyalty, I will allow you to decide this *one* time. I can end the life growing within you right now. Or you can birth the child, who will be born powerless, and then give it away."

Sybella was speechless, she was sure the child would be strong. She had done everything possible to ensure it. "I... my Lord, I..."

"Let me be clear, child. Despite the curse you placed on Ashrek, which is being broken even as we speak. And despite the potion you took to make the child strong, I will make sure it is born deformed and powerless. It will be unwanted by anyone of importance. It will never be given the opportunity to fulfill your hopes."

Sybella closed her mouth in defeat and looked down at her clasped hands, "I understand my Lord. The potion sped up the pregnancy, so I am due to give birth within two weeks' time. I would ask for your patience and understanding. Perhaps my desire to see the child is a weakness that needs to be purged. Forgive me for not consulting you first."

"You are forgiven, and you have two weeks at which time I will demand your complete obedience in this matter. Until that time, confine yourself to your room. I will call if I need you before then. Chumbra, take her away."

"As you wish, my Lord," Chumbra said with another deep bow, satisfaction lacing his every word.

The hallway was silent except for the echoes of their footsteps against the stone floor.

"Not so smug now are you, *Lady Sybella*," Chumbra sneered. "You thought you could march in here and take my place. It won't be that simple. You could never do the things I have done. You are too weak, and now *he* knows it just as I do."

Having arrived at the room she would be confined in, Sybella looked at Chumbra and smiled. "Send the boy to me." Then she closed the door without another word. She listened to the insipid man storm off, muttering under his breath all the while. Turning she found a meager dwelling, the fire was out and the bed unmade. Whoever had stayed here prior to her had left in a hurry. Waving her hands and whispering a few words, a whirlwind swept through the room clearing it of dust and debris. The bedding was replaced with black silks and the fire sprang to life. Lowering herself into the single chair she wrapped her hands around her large belly feeling the child move within her.

Ashrek writhed and screamed in agony as Yasmine continued the chanting, the pressure building and boiling inside his flesh. What felt like hours later he felt a cool wind blow across his exposed back, looking up he saw Yasmine standing by the open window.

"It is done. You are free of the curse and will live," the girl said without turning around.

"And the cost?" Ashrek could feel the difference in his body already, his gift was there but buried. Ashrek gasped as she turned to face him, where flesh had been, now blinked one solitary brown eye, staring back at him from the center of her forehead.

"It has been paid," she said simply, as she walked to the door and exited with his anguished groans floating behind her.

"Sire, the girl! Are you alright?" The captain of the guard stepped hesitantly into the room.

"I will be fine." Ashrek sat partially hidden in shadow, hunched over with a bloody rag wrapped around his face to hide the empty cavity where she'd carved his eye from its socket.

"Bring me some food, water and fresh clothing. Assemble the generals. WE are going to war."

Chapter 5

THE BRANCHES WHIPPED HER IN THE FACE, pulling at her hair and tearing into her skin like clawed fingers. No matter how fast she ran the demon hounds kept getting closer and closer to her heels. The meager amount of food she had scavenged provided little energy, and she was nearing collapse. Her foot caught on an exposed root and she tumbled to the forest floor. The creatures howled their delight and drew closer as she clawed her way forward on bloody knees. Standing she looked over her shoulder just as one lunged towards her, its jaws open with saliva dripping from the sharp teeth. Screaming she fell backwards into a clearing. The creature landed at the edge of the jade grass, furious but either unwilling or unable to pursue her any further.

She collapsed on her back and laughed bitterly as tears streamed down the side of her mud caked face. After taking a few moments to catch her breath, she rubbed her hands into the thick grass on either side of her thin body. It was thick and soft, cushioning her like a fur rug. Her closed eyes fluttered beneath the warmth of the sun and a breeze brushed her scalp exposed through her thinning hair. Pushing to sit up, she looked around her and wondered what paradise she had stumbled into. In the middle of the clearing a single tree stood tall with broad leaves and wide roots, it was from behind this tree that a solitary figure appeared and began walking towards her.

She was not afraid exactly, but she felt nervous. Something was definitely off about the person coming her way. Scrambling to her knees she tried to stand only to fall again as her ankle sent shock waves of pain up her leg.

Do not be afraid. Would you let me look at your ankle? I can help you, if you allow me to.

The voice washed over her like a caress, and she nodded as more tears fell unbidden down her cheeks.

Come, Devona.

"How do you know me?" She gasped as he knelt and placed a warm hand on her ankle, easing the pain instantly.

I know you Devona. I will tell you all about myself if you wish it. Or you can go on your way. The choice will always be yours.

Devona looked at the person before her, she could not determine if it was a man or a woman she saw. All she could conclude was that the entity meant her no harm and after all she had endured, that was more than enough for her.

"You can heal my leg. And if you have any food and water I would appreciate that also." Her words were soft and humble.

Of course. Come with me. The entity offered her a hand to help her up and indicated that she follow along.

"You know my name, so what should I call you?" Devona asked.

You may call me Adi, if you wish.

"Alright Adi, where are we? I thought this forest was dead, cursed a long time ago."

It is dead, but no, it was never cursed. Only hidden from those who no longer deserve to enter. The place you stand now is holy to followers of the light. Darkness cannot enter, as you saw with the demon hounds.

"If that is the case, how is it that I am here? I do not follow the light." Devona said casually.

That is true, you are not of the light. But you have the potential within you, a spark must be there that granted you access. It is up to you whether you nurture the spark or let the darkness blot it out once more.

Devona pondered his words as she was led to a table behind the great tree. Heaped plates of brown rice sat beside steaming flat bread, and the aroma from the stews made her mouth water. Chicken, fish and what may have been venison sat ready for the taking. Her eyes feasted on each item and her stomach rumbled at the sight of the sweets on the very end of the table. Sticky buns and pastries, candied dates and little cake squares. Things she had never seen before let alone tasted sat before her. Each setting was laid with utensils that gleamed and plates with sun rays etched into their rims. The crystal glasses sat ready for the wine in the matching pitchers placed here and there on the long table. Narrowing her eyes, she noted the absence of flies and wondered how it remained fresh, she looked at Adi questioningly.

I am always prepared to feed travelers and those in need of refreshment. Take your fill; I will be there by the stream.

Devona glanced to the place he indicated, she had not even noticed the stream and wondered at its source. Sitting at the table she filled a plate with all sorts of items, most of which she had never seen, but a starving belly does not discriminate. Each bite refreshed her as nothing had before, the best part being the water. It was cool and crisp, with a subtle sweetness to it. When at last she could eat no more, she turned to the river and Adi.

"Has this place always been here?" Devona inquired. Looking around the small glade, it was as if they were encased in a bubble. The place where the dead forest ended and where the grass began was a perfect circle, the large tree standing in its center.

It has been here since the first step of those who search for purpose and will continue until the search is no longer required.

Devona looked at Adi with skepticism, "And have you always been here as well? Or were there others before you?"

I have been, and no there are none before me, nor will there be any other than me. Imposters will come and go, but the truth stands.

"Right. OK, do you have any clothing I can use, and a pack that you wouldn't mind parting with? I would like to continue my journey home. There are things I must rectify." Devona looked in the direction she thought Nuru Manor lay; her mind running through plans and possibilities.

I have all you need Devona, you need only ask.

38

"I did ask. Do you have a home or something near? Somewhere I can change in privacy?" Devona snapped, she was irritated by the way Adi spoke. It was as if every word had a double meaning and she couldn't grasp it fully. Having borne the brunt of so much brutality and subterfuge in the last year she could take no more.

My home has many rooms prepared for any who come to me, come. I will show you.

Adi led Devona around the tree to a wooden door in its trunk. It was inlaid with golden symbols that swirled and reformed before her eyes. He opened it and indicated for her to enter first. Immediately, she was struck by the grandeur. It was as if she had walked into a city made entirely of light, it was so bright she had to squint. She looked behind her for the door but did not find it.

Do not panic Devona, you are not trapped here. Once you are clothed and have provisions for your journey I will lead you out once more.

It was as if he could read her thoughts, but she refused to believe that. It was more likely that her face showed her true feelings. She followed him to a home on a small side street. It was white washed with crystal clear panes in the windows and flowers with colors she could not name sat in wooden boxes beneath each one.

I will leave you for now. There is ample clothing that you will find in the closets. The pantry is stocked with everything for your journey. Take only what you need.

Devona couldn't respond, she was so in awe of what she was seeing. She heard the door close softly behind her as she continued further into the home. The wooden floor gleamed as if it had just been polished, as did every surface she came across. Fresh fruit and flowers sat on a table that could easily seat twelve. Opening the door to the pantry she found a variety of dried fruit, meat and biscuits. On a hook behind the door was a brown sack she would fill with everything she could carry. Turning she walked down a short hallway to the bedroom, a comfortably made bed sat in the middle of the room with a white spread on it. The same golden pattern from the door was embroidered into it. A wooden chest sat against the opposite wall where she found clothes for every season folded on its shelves. There were two sides in the chest, one held white clothing and the other held gray. Devona hesitated for only a moment before selecting a gray woolen tunic and matching breeches. She had not been accustomed to wearing men's clothing but the rough journey in her torn skirts had given her wisdom. Her eye fell on a lamp positioned near a wash basin. It was filled with oil and would come in handy for night travel.

Having washed and changed clothing she returned to the main room and ate her fill before filling the sack with as much food stuff as it would hold. A soft knock on the door alerted her to Adi's return.

Are you ready? Adi gave her a brief glance, and for a moment it was as if he were disappointed with her choices.

"Yes, I am." Devona shouldered the bag and exited the home. Together they made their way to the main street where the wooden door stood open once again.

Devona, I hope you will consider my words. Darkness hides many pitfalls. It would pain me if you were lost to it. Adi walked with her through the door and to the edge of the glade.

"I will Adi, but not now. First I must return to my son and right the wrongs done to me." Devona took a step forward, one foot in the dead forest, one foot in the glade. "Will the hounds attack me once I leave?"

As long as you stay on the path, they will not.

"Alright." She hesitated for a moment before asking, "Can I return once I have completed all that I need to do?"

Adi looked at her with compassion. *The glade is here for all who seek it. Only be warned, no man knows when his journey will end and seeking will no longer be possible. Do it while you have the time.*

Devona nodded, she had more pressing things to do now. Turning, she stepped onto the path and headed for the manor. She would pay them all back, son or not, David would pay for the hell he had put her through.

Chapter 6

ALRIC WOKE WITH A START, having felt the familiar nudging in his mind. He left the home and walked to the river's edge. Sitting with his legs crossed and eyes closed he waited for The One to speak to him.

Alric, one is coming who you must allow into your midst. She is important to the tapestry of the prophecy. You must convince the others of this.

"Who is she?" Alric asked.

One who is at a crossroads.

"I will do as you say." Alric sat for a few moments as the atmosphere around him returned to normal. "Good morning, Laney."

Without opening his eyes he knew she sat just to his right, watching and waiting.

Shaking her head, Elainea laughed. "What did The One have to say this time? Did he change his mind about the prophecy perhaps?"

Alric stood and stretched, then helped his sister to stand. "No, you are still destined to boss me around."

"I had to ask. So what was the message?" Elainea asked.

"Someone is coming that we will need to fulfill the prophecy. A woman. I don't know who and I don't know when. I was told to convince you all of her importance." Alric watched chunks of ice floating down the river.

"That doesn't sound good at all." The last thing they all needed was an unknown factor in their midst. The group from the south that Keuri had summoned should be showing up any day, she said they were all on the same side, but who can really tell the true intentions of a person's heart. "Let's get back. We need to speak with Akronius and the others about strategy once all the southerners arrive."

A cold wind blew in from the north as the pair made their way back to the home. The first flakes fell and melted on Elainea's red hair.

"You two are up early." Akronius said, from where he sat on a stump placed by the door. "Anything we need to know about?"

"Better to wait for the others so everyone can hear it at the same time. It's nothing bad, in my opinion, but new information nonetheless." Alric turned and shielded his eyes as the wind picked up unexpectedly, buffeting them all ruthlessly. Swirling his hands quickly he encompassed his sister and Akronius within a shield. From the corner of his eye he could see his father step to the doorway and the others emerged from the barn, fighting against the wind. All except Keuri, who smiled and waved it away.

"THEY ARE HERE!" she shouted. As she forced the wind to obey her command, a large group of people could be seen heading

43

their way. At the front stood a man covered in so many furs that only his green eyes were visible.

"Admit it Keuri, I almost had you that time." The man said once he was close enough.

"Not even close, Lorenz." The two embraced, clapping each other roughly on the back.

"Everyone, this is Lorenz. My weaker older brother. Lorenz, this is Akronius. Kaison. Elainea. And Alric." Keuri introduced everyone by nodding at them.

"Ah, the would-be king." Lorenz said, inspecting Alric closely.

"Not anymore. There is quite a bit we all need to speak about," Keuri answered. "First we need to get everyone settled, and then the leaders will gather and discuss plans for attack."

"So soon?" Lorenz asked in surprise.

"As I said, much to discuss," Keuri responded.

Everyone pitched in to get the southerners settled in the tents they had brought, there were easily a thousand people present. Alric was surprised that so many would venture into an unknown war supporting an unknown claim to a throne they swore no allegiance to. Yet he knew it was the threat of David and the Dark Lord that brought them together, and once that threat was eliminated, they would return to their homes.

It took the entire day for the newly founded camp to settle in. Once they did, Keuri called the generals to meet with Alric and the others around a fire.

Akronius eyed the five newcomers, before nodding at Keuri for introductions. "This is Karl, he is our main strategist. He is brilliant, as long as you can ignore his arrogance. Beside him is Marx, put any sharp object in his hand, give him a target and he won't miss. Then the twins William and Quilliana, he is fire to her ice. Lastly, is our oracle Lorox, physically he is blind but his sight has come in handy more times than I care to remember."

Lorox spoke into the short silence that followed the introductions. "Well met." His voice was deep and resonated with power. He turned his face towards Alric. "You are very strong for one so young. The glow of The One lingers around you. What name do you go by?

"Alric."

"You are destined for more than a kingship." Lorox stated.

"Yes, that is true. The prophecy, in its entirety says, '***When the dead King returns, darkness will follow. Evil will fill places left hollow. One throne, one life, one death to claim, one to alter, one to change. The One to judge the two between, no pawn, no rook, no bishop nor king.'*** We understand it to mean Elainea will be queen. I have been given a different path." When Alric finished speaking gasps and murmurs rose around him.

Lorox raised a hand and silenced them. "I agree with this interpretation."

"Now that we have that settled, we must speak about strategy. We know David will be planning an attack, as will the lords of Vimeo and Arcana, though they may have joined forces by now." Akronius said gazing into the fire.

"We should send a scout to find out for sure. It will be a waste of resources to plan for three battles if there may only be one or two," Karl interjected. "I will send one of my runners in the morning to see to it."

Akronius nodded in agreement. "How are your people set up? Will they follow directions from Keuri alone? We need a clear chain of command with such a large number of warriors."

"The group is divided into battalions of 100, they report to one captain who reports to one of these generals." Keuri reported, nodding to the men and women around her. "So each general is responsible for two captains and 200 warriors. They all possess either gifts or tactical prowess that will aid us in the coming battles."

Just as Kaison was about to respond, Lorox once again raised his hand for silence. "We are not alone." The group fell silent but alert, searching the area around them with their eyes.

"You are shrouded in darkness, but I see you. Step into the light," commanded Lorox. As one, the group stood and readied their weapons. Each faced outward into the night, unsure if the unseen person was a threat or an ally.

A woman's voice was heard from just outside the fire light. "Accept my apologies for sneaking up on you all like this. Will you guarantee my safety if I reveal myself? I could be an ally in exchange for assurance of my safety in doing so."

"You have it." Alric responded immediately, having felt the 'inner-nudging' once again the moment he heard the feminine voice.

"Thank you, young sir." Slowly a form became visible, a thin frame and stringy black hair pulled into a harsh ponytail surrounded piercing dark brown eyes. The woman looked around the circle until her gaze fell on Kaison. Her heart stopped the instant their eyes met, for she had thought him dead!

"I'LL KILL YOU!" Kaison roared, trying to leap across the flames with hands reaching for her throat.

Chaos ensued as the others tried to restrain the livid ex-king. Never had they seen Kaison lose control as he did in that moment. So much so, that Lorox was forced to intervene. He placed one hand on Kaison's chest. "Peace," he hushed over the outraged man. The others watched as Kaison dropped limply into their arms. Karl and William carried the unconscious man into the house, as the others turned to face the woman whose arrival had caused the disturbance.

"Who are you?" Keuri demanded, pointing her sword at the stranger.

Akronius answered through gritted teeth. "Her name is Devona. In another life I was her accomplice and helped her betray

Kaison and murder his wife - Alric's mother. Why are you here Devona?"

"Nice to see you again as well, Akronius," Devona smirked. "I escaped imprisonment in Arcana. Ashrek is now lord of the manor and its surrounding region. I am unsure if he killed Sybella but he did kill her father, Lord Vicrano."

"I asked why you are *here*. Not how you journeyed." Akronius repeated, his patience thinning.

"She has been sent by The One to assist us in fulfilling the prophecy." Alric responded as he inspected the woman before him. His sight told him she was hiding something, but the conversation from his morning meditation replayed in his mind. "We must accept her aid."

"Alric, you do not know this woman. She cannot be trusted. She had your mother killed! For all we know she is the reason your father was imprisoned for years! How can you accept her now?" Akronius was shocked and a bit disgusted.

"YOU killed my mother Akronius! Yet here you are, with my full forgiveness and trust. My father fights by your side as a brother. The very woman, whose children you were sent to kill, accepted you into her home and treated you as a son. Would you withhold the same forgiveness from another? Is she any less deserving than you?" Alric spoke gently, his words probing and straight to the heart of the matter.

"I…" Akronius looked at Devona with loathing, and then pity. "No, I would not begrudge her forgiveness. I would dishonor The One in doing so. But know this woman, I will be watching every move you make."

"I would expect no less from you Akronius. And for the record, I had no idea Chumbra had kept him alive. I thought he was dead." Devona dipped her head. "But that is all in the past now isn't it? During my escape, I happened upon the most glorious place in the forbidden wood. I was met by someone called Adi, and experienced something I find hard to put into words. I am no longer the same woman you knew so long ago, Akronius. I promise you that."

"Time will tell." Akronius replied before he stalked off into the night.

"In this place you found, was there a large tree?" Alric questioned her.

"YES! You have been there?" Devona questioned.

"Yes, I spent some time there. I learned much about myself and my purpose. Did you experience the same enlightenment?" Alric watched her face seeking the truth.

"I wouldn't call it enlightenment, but I certainly left better than I arrived." Devona confirmed.

"Yes, I did as well. In a manner of speaking." Alric studied her silently for a moment. "Tell me Devona, do you know about the prophecy?"

"Everyone knows of the prophecy, nephew. **When the dead King returns, darkness will follow. Evil will fill places left hollow. One throne, one life, one death to claim, one to alter, one to change.** Or something like that." Devona waved her hand as if dismissing the words.

"Yes, Devona. Something like that." Alric smiled. Those who remained around the fire looked at him but said nothing, following his lead in how much was revealed to the woman in gray. "It is late, let's get you settled into a tent and tomorrow we can discuss how you can help in fulfilling the prophecy."

"Thank you, Alric. That sounds wonderful." Devona said as she followed the young man away from the fire, while watchful eyes remained trained on her back.

"We cannot wait for David to gather his full strength. We must attack now, while we hold the element of surprise!"

Ashrek sat back in his chair, hands tented before his face, watching his generals argue back and forth across the map about the best course of action. "ENOUGH!" The sound of his palm colliding with the wooden table reverberated around the room. He had regained much of his strength in the week since the witch had removed the curse, taking his eye as payment. He wore a patch to hide the empty socket and it enhanced his already angry countenance. "We will do nothing until the scout returns with word from my uncle on how many men he will be sending to join us."

As if he had been called by name, the door opened and a pock-faced boy entered the room. He was a gangly youth who had proven adept at blending in and gathering information without being seen. "Sire, your uncle, Lord Alcherist, has promised 300 men for the coming battle. He said he will meet you on the field."

"Very good. NOW, we can plan for the battle." Ashrek dismissed the boy with a wave and turned back to his generals. "David has Sybella at his side. She is a powerful and shrewd woman. Though she can no longer transport herself from place to place, she still has access to dark magic and spells. If she is partnered with the oracle Chumbra, who is just as depraved as she, they will be a formidable force. We must find a way to break them apart. Destroy them from the inside as we attack from the outside."

The generals leaned over the table, hanging on his every word as their plans began to take shape.

Chapter 7

THE SUN WAS JUST BEGINNING TO SET as Chumbra sauntered down the hall towards David's room. The wretched woman was still sequestered in her quarters and was of no use to anyone in her condition. He had been skeptical at first, but now he was sure she posed no threat. Of course they would have to find a way to work together, but they could be an unstoppable force as they followed the Dark Lord to victory and unimaginable power.

"You summoned me, my Lord." Chumbra lowered his head slightly.

"Yes. The battle is about to begin and I need your help to prepare the grounds." David said, his eyes dark, like bottomless pits.

"Anything you need. I can bring the maps and show you the best location to draw battle lines, in places where we will have the most advantage."

"I do not need maps." David said smoothly.

"Of course, my apologies." Chumbra cowered for the briefest of moments.

"Has the town surrounding the manor been emptied of all dissenters?"

"Well, yes, err well almost. There are a few hold-outs left. I have convinced most to fall in line and bend the knee to your rule," Chumbra said with a hint of pride.

"Perfect. Follow me." David stood and walked out of the room, Chumbra close on his heels.

Together they walked out of the manor and to the outskirts of the town. Stopping just outside the gates David drew a blade from beneath his cloak, grabbed Chumbra by the arm, and in one smooth motion slit his throat. The garnet colored liquid flowed down the front of Chumbra's tunic, staining it and filling the grooves between the cobblestones as it ran down the road. Chumbra wrapped his hands around his neck in a vain attempt to stem the flow. His eyes were wide with unbelief as he stared into the dismissive eyes of his master.

David's smile was wide. He chanted and waved his arms over the sanguine fluid mixing with the mud, creating a thick sludge that oozed between the stones and into the crevices. From it burst flames that attached to the barrels and pieces of wood left strewn about as if they had a life of their own, from the street to the houses and abandoned stalls of the marketplace. In only a few moments all the houses nearest him were completely engulfed in flames, if any of the remaining villagers fleeing for their lives had tried they would find it impossible to extinguish them. With a flick of his wrist, he lifted the body of Chumbra in the air and tossed it into the nearest blaze as if it were no more than a bag of discarded fruit peelings. Turning back to the manor, the screams of the villagers left behind began to filter into the air as they ran for their lives. Those loyal to him had already been moved into a different part of the town and would be spared the conflagration.

From a window set high in the manor, Sybella watched David return through the gates as the town burned, rubbing her large belly lost in thought. A short time later, the sun rose through a smoky haze, the cold breeze that blew through Sybella's open window carried the scent of death and snow. She felt the child move inside her and knew her time was closer than she thought. She would need to set a few things in place before the baby dropped into the world. Opening the door she made to call for Jacob, only to find his small body curled at the base of the door. *Chumbra allowed his servants to be treated abysmally*, she thought as she nudged the boy with her foot.

"Wake up boy, I need water." Her heart may have been softening with the progression of her pregnancy, but she would not let anyone else know that. Fear was still the best motivator.

"Yes at once, mistress." Jacob scurried down the hall wiping the sleep from his eyes.

Once he returned, Sybella watched as he lit the fire to warm the frigid pot of water, she could have done it herself but she needed him to feel useful if her plans were to work.

"What was your name again?" She inquired.

"Jacob, mistress."

54

"Ah yes. That's right," Sybella cooed. "You are entrusted to Chumbra correct?"

"Yes, I serve him and anyone he sends me to." Jacob answered.

"You will be serving only me from now on. I will advise Chumbra of the change when he finds the time to visit me." Sybella shifted position in the chair she was reclining in.

"As you wish, mistress. Shall, I fetch your breakfast now?" Jacob stood by the door, hands clasped before him, eyes downcast.

"In a few moments." Sybella looked at the boy closely, his skin was ashen and his hair filthy. The nails on both hands were bitten down to nubs, blood and dirt mixed on the tips of boney fingers. The clothing he wore had more holes than seams, the britches revealed at least three inches of his thin ankle which sat above boots with no laces: His dirty stocking clad toes visible through the tip of one. He shifted self-consciously at her obvious perusal and disdain of his appearance.

"I'll need you to bring more water for a bath. You must better fit the role you will be playing as my servant."

"Mistress, that is not allowed... I'm to bathe in the barn. The servants take turns once a month." Jacob risked a glance up in shock and humiliation.

"I am your mistress now, and you will do as I say, Jacob. Do not question my wishes again. What you are used to will be no more." Sybella dismissed him, leaning back against the cushions and closing her eyes.

"As you wish." Jacob said. Closing the door behind him he wondered what game she was playing, kindness was never given without a cost. He hurried down to the kitchens, passing Chumbra's room as he went. Peeking in he wondered where the man was, he hadn't seen him since he'd been sent by him to wait on Sybella the previous evening. *Probably off torturing more people in that dungeon of his,* Jacob thought. It was just as well, he had no desire to return to being in service to that oracle. Sybella was said to be evil incarnate, so far he had seen no signs of that being true, still he would keep his guard up.

Having reached the kitchen he enlisted the help of two kitchen girls to carry large buckets of hot water to the room under the guise of Sybella wishing to bathe, no need to draw unwanted attention to himself over some soap and water. Jacob felt the dark watchful eyes of Sybella following him as he poured each bucket into the tub she had stationed behind a screen. Turning, he was unsure of how to proceed, surely she did not intend to stay and watch him bathe.

Sensing his discomfort, Sybella rolled her eyes but drew the heavy drapes surrounding the bed she lay in, giving the poor boy a semblance of privacy. "Bathe quickly and then you will assist me down to the kitchens. I do not trust the cooks here to prepare my meals just yet."

"Yes, mistress," Jacob's response was barely a whisper as he dropped his clothing on the floor and stepped into the steaming water. Picking up the small piece of soap he inhaled its scent, it was nothing compared to the lavender scented baths his mother had given him. The memory brought tears to his eyes and he fought to restrain them. Scrubbing until his brown skin gleamed, every nook and cranny, every nail was spotless, he hoped his mother would be proud. She had always made sure they were clean and fed. He missed her, he missed them all. He allowed a solitary tear to fall, watching as it hit the murky lukewarm water before standing and wrapping a thick towel around his frame.

"Uh Mistress... where are my clothes?" Jacob looked around quickly, his eyes glancing over a pile of folded clothing on a bench nearby.

"They're on the bench. Put those on. The other rags have been burned." Sybella's voice carried from the shadows behind him.

Taking a step forward his jaw dropped as he lifted the linen shirt in one hand, the other still clutched the towel close. The coarse fabric did not have one sign of wear on it. The britches were crafted from animal hide and would provide more warmth than he had known in months! There were also new stockings and thickly soled boots with laces. The pressure in his chest built until he could scarcely breathe. Drying off as quickly as he could, he pulled each item on with great care. Stepping from behind the screen he saw Sybella sitting on the edge of the bed.

"That is yours as well." She indicated a black woolen cape thrown across the back of the chair. "There will be a cot brought into this room by the end of the day, and you will have a trunk with a spare set of clothing. Take care of these gifts, my generosity has limits."

"Yes, Mistress. Thank you very much. I will take care of them, all of them. I swear it!" Jacob gushed.

Sybella smiled as she watched the first brick in his wall fall. "Now, I need you to gather a few things for me."

Chapter 8

SHAMA STOOD ON A SMALL OUTCROPPING of rocks, a ledge on which very few would have the courage to set foot. It extended out from the mountain and hovered in the air surrounded by misty clouds, here he waited in silence; his staff in one hand and a small pack at his feet. The faintest shift in the air current was all the warning he received as large feathered wings blew the clouds back, revealing golden eyes and lethal talons. The large eagle landed silently and stayed perfectly still as Shama climbed aboard its broad back. With one step they plummeted down the face of the mountain, the great bird's wings tucked into its side, Shama desperately clinging on. With a loud SNAP the bird extended its wings, halting their downward descent, swooping back up towards the dawn-flushed sky.

"Ha ha ha! Rafa, that was thrilling, my old friend!" Shama exclaimed. "It has been too long since we last flew together."

Rafa let a shrill cry of agreement pierce the early morning silence. Leveling them off, the golden eagle rode the currents with ease.

"We must be swift. You know where we are heading. Let's Ride the wind!" Shama whispered, leaning forward as they turned and headed south, for the farm.

Kaison sat on a boulder near the almost frozen river, chunks of ice moving slowly down the frigid current. He couldn't stand to be near the others, all but Akronius welcomed that... that... *woman* with open arms! He couldn't understand it. The sound of her voice grated on his nerves so badly in the days since her arrival he had taken to staying alone as often as possible. He felt more than saw the moment Naia approached his side. *You are troubled by the woman. She smells like you.*

"Yes, she is... was my sister." Kaison said, running his hand through Naia's thick winter coat.

Was? She is alive, Kaison. Naia responded softly.

"Yes, but she is dead to me. She murdered my wife, my mate." Bitterness rang through his words, creeping across their bond, eliciting a growl from the Dire Wolf.

She is evil then. Why has Alric allowed her to remain? Naia questioned.

"He said The One instructed him to. That she has a purpose to serve in the fulfillment of the prophecy."

Naia was silent for a moment, she understood how the instructions of The One could seem to make no sense. *I am sorry for your pain. The One's ways are different from our own. His plans are higher than our understanding. We must be patient and trust all will be revealed in time. But, should you need me, I will not hesitate to rip her throat out.*

Kaison smiled for the first time in days. "Thank you my friend. I will try not to ask that of you, though the thought had crossed my mind even before you offered. Still, I would not want your taste to be offended by one so bitter."

The chuff could only be interpreted as a wolfish laugh, as Naia walked back towards the other wolves who patrolled the grounds. The southerners had been struck dumb when the huge wolves first wandered freely among their tents, they were fearsome beasts to be sure. As Kaison stood and surveyed the sea of tents before him, a large shadow crossed his vision. Glancing to the other side, he saw Akronius with Syphra, what could be so large and approaching so swiftly!

"ALRIC!" Kaison bellowed, drawing his sword in preparation. They had been practicing with his shielding abilities, in the hopes that should an attack catch them by surprise, he would be able to cast a shield over the whole company. With barely a nod, Alric emerged from the house arms already in motion. The blue light flew in a wide arc from his outstretched arms, encompassing almost the whole camp. There were maybe ten tents outside his range; it would have to be enough. Kaison watched his son strain to hold the shield, sweat began to drip into his eyes, but he did not give in as the creature drew closer.

A shrill cry pierced the morning and Alric's eyes lit up as he dropped his arms in relief. He recognized that cry, he had heard it only once before but he would never forget it.

"It's alright father! It is a friend!" Alric jogged to join his father by the river. "It is an eagle from the forbidden forest." The excitement in his eyes was apparent as more of their core group gathered by the river and watched the bird approach.

"Hello my friends!" A voice called from behind the white plumed head that dipped to reveal its rider.

Akronius walked forward to greet the man. "Shama! We were not expecting you. Is everything alright?"

"Yes, yes. Everything is as fine as it can be in times like this. I had to come at once, you see I found my old staff, and suddenly things long forgotten became clear. The prophecy I am afraid is not what I led you to believe." He said this looking deeply into Alric's eyes.

"No, it is not. And we are all fine with it as it stands." Akronius said quickly, for Devona had joined them and he still did not trust her fully.

"What do you mean? How could you know that…" Shama began.

"Walk with me." Alric interrupted him. They couldn't have Shama divulging secrets meant to be kept hidden.

Shama raised one eyebrow, but fell in step beside Alric. "You have changed much since we last spoke, young man."

Alric chuckled. "Yes Shama I have. That change would not have taken place if not for your eagle friend, at least partially."

"Rafa? You met... you've been to the glade!" Shama stopped and clapped Alric on the shoulder.

"I have," Alric smiled back. "It was more than I could have imagined and everything I never knew I needed."

"So you know the truth of the prophecy?" Shama said as they continued walking by the river, their breath puffing in the cold air.

"Yes, and we have all made peace with it. Elainea is having the most trouble with it."

"That is to be expected." Shama looked at Alric from the side of his eye, "Have you no questions about it? No, doubts?"

"No, The One has calmed my doubts. There are still fears of the unknown, but I trust the process now. I do wonder how the transition will go." They came to a standstill and stood by a small inlet in the river bank, the ground had been covered in a fine dusting of snow but the glitter of rainbow colored stones twinkled in the sunlight.

"I remember my own transition, I too was uncertain of how it would happen. The one who came before me did not reveal what would happen and neither will I. I cannot prepare you for what I do not know. All I can say is, when you take your place, my knowledge will pass to you along with the knowledge of all those that came before me. It is both a heavy weight and a tremendous honor. You are not an oracle by nature, but you have been chosen."

"Thank you Shama, your faith in me is humbling. I will try every day to live up to your legacy."

"Bah, you'll do fine boy. Now explain to me who that woman in our midst is and why no one wants her to know the true prophecy?" They kept close together and spoke with hushed voices as they began the walk back.

Chapter 9

DEVONA WATCHED THE CAMP WAKE SLOWLY, she was among them but not part of them. Kaison still looked through her as if she did not even exist, and really if she were honest, she could not hold it against him. She had committed the ultimate betrayal in his eyes, maybe one day he would forgive her, and if not forgive her then at least understand her reasons for doing what she did. Though she had thought him dead all this time, it warmed a small part of her heart to see it was not so.

Alric and the old man came back from their secret walk and she narrowed her eyes at them, she knew who he was and she wondered what he had been stopped from saying. It must be something important for them all to want to keep her in the dark. She felt pressure on the back of her head and turned to meet the glare of her brother. Neither was willing to look away first, to be the one to give in, luckily a howl from the snow-laden forest took the choice from them as everyone turned to see what the alert was for.

Nguvu came trotting from the tree line heading for Alric, who stood with the core group and the new generals.

I tracked the man and woman to the large dwelling where the evil king resides. The entire area smells of death and there are very few humans in the streets. There is a bad feeling in the air, something is not right, he said. Kaison translated for the benefit of those standing around

"It is as we feared. Chumbra and Sybella are now working with David. That is a great deal of power in one place. Will we be able to defeat them all?" Elainea asked.

Alric replied. "We have no choice. That evil must not be allowed to remain in our land or spread to any others. We must tear it out at the root. Have faith sister."

"It's not faith I lack," Elainea replied. "It is plans and backup plans. Do we meet them at the manor or do we wait for them to attack us? Do we try to sneak in and take him out quietly? Do we send our best in first, or do we hold them back as reserves? Do we..."

"STOP!" Akronius shouted and then repeated softly, "Stop." To soften the command he took a step closer to her and placed his hand on her shoulder. "What good does all this worrying do? We have the blessing of The One fighting for us, with us. Who can stand against us? All the planning in the world will do nothing if we do not consult the one guiding us and ask for direction."

Akronius looked around at the band of leaders who in turn looked to him before focusing on Alric. "Alric, can you and Shama inquire of The One for guidance? The battle we face will be difficult at best and deadly at worst, we need to make sure our first steps are the right ones."

Alric nodded and once again headed off with Shama as the generals closed ranks, filing into the farmhouse that seemed to grow even smaller as the months passed and their numbers grew.

Devona walked silently at the back of the group but stopped when a hand blocked her at the doorway.

"You're not needed here." Akronius hissed, and then watched as she stalked back to her tent before closing the door.

Elainea rekindled the fire and started preparing dough for bread, finding comfort in the mundane activity. Her mind roamed to the many possible outcomes as she added water to the flour and began kneading it. Her hands moved on their own, muscle memory from years of preparing bread, rolls and cakes with her mother. *Mother,* a tear rolled down her cheek and landed on the cream colored mound before her, *I could really use your advice right now. I miss you so much.* No one spoke as the fire spread its warmth throughout the small room. Bodies occupied every chair and the rest leaned against walls or sat on the floor, each lost in their own thoughts of the future.

Keuri broke the silence. "Think you'll ever be finished kneading that dough? I would really like some bread to go with my misery."

"What? Oh, sorry." Elainea set the dough to rise under a cloth and turned to face the rest of the room. "So, what do we do next?"

"We plan while we wait for word from Alric." Akronius said, leaning forward onto the wooden table. "We know David and

Chumbra have been plotting this for a very long time, Sybella is the unknown factor. We have to wait to hear from the scout we sent out on what is going on in Arcana and Vimeo."

"He should be back within a day or two," Keuri responded. "While we wait, can we discuss how to present Elainea as the intended Queen, or are you planning to simply spring that on the people at the end of everything?"

Elainea glared at Keuri, the woman could be absolutely infuriating. "And HOW do you propose we do that? Can you train me in the ways of the court? Will I suddenly gain all the knowledge and feminine wiles you mentioned I lacked?"

Keuri smiled sweetly. "No. But there is suddenly someone in our midst who *could* do all those things." She glanced at Akronius. "Her timing couldn't have been better really."

"Absolutely not! I forbid it." Kaison stated firmly. "She is only skilled in betrayal! That is not something anyone needs to learn."

Lorox turned his head to one side slightly, "Perhaps you should consider this. She couldn't always have been as she is now. I am sure as children you both received the finest education, and she surely learned lessons of more refinement that were not required of you. Alric told us an ally would come, a *female* ally. He believes she was sent by The One, and we have come to trust his judgment. Or has that changed?"

"He's right Kaison." Akronius agreed. "As much as I'd prefer to send her on her way, she is the only person who can help us with this part. We don't have to like her, we will continue to watch her, but at least we can use her."

"Do what you will. I want nothing to do with her." Kaison stood to leave. "When you are prepared to speak of battle, call me." He paused looking at each person in the room. "I hope you do not regret this."

"Well, Keuri, this was your idea," Lorenz said with a smirk. "Go get her."

Keuri rolled her eyes but obeyed. She walked slowly towards the tent of the woman so many hated. "Hello!" She called.

Devona's pale face peeked out from the tent's flap, eyeing the short woman before her. "Yes, what do you want?"

Keuri was beginning to understand why the woman was so easy to dislike. "We need your help with something. Come back to the house with me, and we can explain the plan to you."

Devona raised one eyebrow. "Really? Well then, let's go." Gathering her shawl she followed behind the woman. As they entered the house, conversations halted and the air thickened with a mixture of distrust and curiosity.

"Devona, we need your assistance with something." Akronius began, shifting his gaze from Alric to meet Devona's dark eyes. "This would be a good way to begin earning our trust."

"Of course, Akronius. What would you have me do?" Devona asked, keeping her face as bland as possible as she looked around the room at the many faces.

"As you know, Alric is heir to the throne you and your son have usurped. As such, he has indicated his sister will remain at his side." Akronius said, tilting his head in Elainea's direction.

"Naturally." Devona replied.

"Yes, well. She will need some instruction in the ways of the court. Seeing as you were raised a princess, you seem ideal for this role." Akronius looked to Elainea as he finished making his appeal to see her flushing uncomfortably.

Devona followed his gaze to the young woman standing awkwardly under the scrutiny of a dozen eyes. Narrowing her own in concentration, she was sure something else was going on. But what?

Chapter 10

SHAMA AND ALRIC SAT WITH LEGS CROSSED and hands resting gently on their laps, they had been sitting in this same pose for the last few hours waiting patiently for direction from The One. Through slits in his eyes Shama observed the young man before him, no not a young man anymore. Alric had grown in the time they were apart, dark stubble shaded the strong jaw and though the hair remained untamed there was stillness and confidence in his stature now. Shama was proud of the man Alric had become and was beginning to understand why he had been chosen as his replacement. He was humble minded and had no desire for wealth or gain, outside of a full belly of course, and even in that, his sense of humor would be needed in the many years he would have ahead of him. It was true what was said about The One, his ways truly were unknowable to mere men and often confusing, but always right.

The fire had dwindled to embers and a chill was creeping under the folds of the tent, Shama was prepared to give up for the night and started to stretch his limbs when a breeze drifted around the space sending chills racing across his skin and the hairs on the back of his neck raised. Alric inhaled deeply, lifting his head as the breeze slid around him and into the fire causing it to blaze anew. Both men opened their eyes and found themselves transported to the glade where before them stood a corporeal image of the one they beseeched.

Shama, Alric. It is good to speak with you again. I have watched and waited for the right moment to make my plans known to you. What would you ask?

"Adi, we are on the verge of war. The woman you said would come to aid us is here, though many do not trust her. David and Chumbra have joined forces with Sybella and we suspect Ashrek will either march against them or us or both. We are in desperate need of your guidance." Alric stated calmly. Though there was urgency in his request, there was no fear in his voice.

Turning to Shama, Adi waited before speaking. *"And what would you ask?"*

Shama took a moment to consider what it was he needed to know. It was true he needed guidance to help with the attack but when he looked deeper inside he knew there was more and it was for this question he knew that Adi waited. "Will it hurt?"

From the corner of his eye, Shama could see the dark brows of Alric draw together in confusion and then look again to Adi. *Only for a moment.*

Shama nodded and straightened his shoulders, he would be ready.

"Adi, what do you mean?" Alric asked.

The question was not yours and neither is the answer. Be at peace Alric. When the time comes, you will understand. As for the war, it will rage for generations to come. This is only one battle, great though it will be, I will guide you. And if you and those who fight with you are willing to give their all, you will be victorious.

Alric felt his heart stutter in his chest, he knew the battle would be fierce and many would give their lives to the cause. He could only hope and pray the ones he loved most would not be counted among the lost.

The three armies will meet on the battlefield. Brother will be against sister, fathers against their children. Friends will become enemies and salvation will come from the skies. Shama, in your possession is something that must be passed on, it is missing a part that will turn the tide of the battle. You must discover what that is. Alric when you hold it, you must not hesitate to use it.

Shama knew Adi spoke of the staff but did not know what part was missing from it; he would need to meditate on it. It must lie in his memories somewhere, hidden like the staff had been for so long. Alric watched as Shama became lost in his thoughts, pondering what Adi had revealed. Still the question remained, where would the battle take place and when?

"Adi..." Alric began.

The battle will take place when day is as night. In one week you must be prepared to march, and when dawn does not break, you will know that you have arrived.

Alric felt the first tendrils of fear trying to claw its way into his mind. He had never known war, never had a real fight even with fists. He thought he was prepared, but hearing the finality in Adi's voice he realized he had never fully grasped the enormity of it till this very moment. His mind called forth images of blood and the pain-filled cries of his sister and the people who had come to support them. Squeezing his eyes shut he could feel his shoulders begin to curve inward, trying to escape the onslaught of voices. His chest constricted as he tried to inhale and his palms became slick and trembled as he rubbed them on the leg of his britches.

Peace.

The word spoken in a whisper wrapped itself around Alric's soul and eased the tension in his muscles, gradually his fears came under subjection and he was able to straighten under the weight of the now certain future. *Be strong and courageous. I have told you and chosen you for this task. I will not abandon you. Will you be faithful?*

"We will." Alric and Shama said in unison as the glade faded from view.

Kaison knelt just inside the tent, watching and waiting, barely breathing as he felt the weight of the atmosphere. The air was sweetly scented and swirled gently around the three of them. Alric and Shama sat with eyes open and fixed on an unseen image, both sets glowing brightly. Alric's momentarily dimmed but then burst forth stronger than Shama's, causing Kaison to wonder what had happened in the vision they shared. As the presence lifted from the tent Kaison heard a voice floating into his mind. *Forgive her as you forgave him.* Kaison shuddered and felt the tears leak from the corners of his eyes as he bowed his head in submission of the gentle but firm rebuke. It would be hard, but the will of The One was strong enough to carry him through.

"Father, are you alright?" Alric asked, as he stretched and rose with Shama

"Yes, son. Yes. I will be fine. What have you learned?" Kaison asked, as he also rose and swiped his hands across his face.

"Come we need to meet with all the generals and discuss what we have been told." Shama said. He could tell Kaison had also had an experience as they sat entranced. The spirit moved where it willed and seldom left any receptive soul untouched.

As the trio walked through the throng of tents the setting sun cast a soft glow on the horizon, fires were lit and friends huddled together, casting watchful eyes on the shaman. Though laughter could be heard it was clear everyone was holding their breaths, waiting for word on where and when the battle would begin.

Entering the small home first, Alric burst into laughter, causing Elainea to jump and drop the cup she was daintily holding to her lips. The other generals must have retired for the evening and only the woman remained. The expression on his sister's face clearly indicated whatever they were doing she found tortuous.

"My Lady." Alric bowed at the waist still chuckling, causing Keuri to look down in order to hide the grin spreading across her own face.

"Shut up, you. This is *all* your fault you know." Elainea stood away from the table and nearly tripped over the dress she was wearing. Alric straightened solemnly and approached her. "Was this mother's? You look beautiful in it. Uncomfortable, but beautiful. She would have loved to see you like this."

Kaison entered the room and it was as if the air was knocked from his lungs. Elainea stood looking every bit the queen. The jade fabric of the dress floated around her and brought tears to his eyes.

Brushing her hand down the silky fabric Elainea sighed. "We found it in mother's chest. I never knew she had such finery. It is a bit long, so I'm not sure if she ever wore it."

"That is because the dress belonged to Alanna. It must have been in the bag she packed the night she ran from…" Glancing at his sister he was shocked to see her pale a bit as she too recalled the night she ordered the death of her sister-in-law. He walked until he stood close enough to touch the fabric and smiled sadly.

"It looks stunning on you Elainea. Befitting a queen." Kaison whispered, placing a kiss on her forehead. "Devona will be a good teacher for you. She always excelled at court when we were young. She will teach you all you need to know, I am sure."

Devona could only stare, her lips parted in shock at the praise her brother gave her. What had happened to bring about such a change in attitude?

"I will go gather the generals." Kaison said as he turned to go back out into the cold evening. Shama patted his shoulder as he walked by, smiling in understanding.

By the time the men had all returned, night had fully fallen and a cold wind was blowing through the camp. Alric wasted no time in relaying the message from Adi.

"We must prepare the men to leave immediately. Adi said we would march until day is as dark as night and once that happens wherever we are - will be the place the battle will occur."

Each general nodded and returned to inform the captains and allow the word to pass through the ranks of men and women. Battle was coming sooner than any had thought. Moving faster than any desired.

Keuri sat with Elainea as the others left until once again only the women remained in the room. "Devona, thank you for your help. We can do some more training tomorrow if you are available." Elainea mumbled. However reluctant she was to learn these skills, she knew it was a necessary evil.

"Of course. I'll see you in the morning." Devona rose and glanced at Keuri who remained seated. "Have I graduated from needing an escort?"

"It would appear so. Still, it would be best if you went straight to your tent. Nothing good happens to those who prefer shadows." Keuri confirmed.

"Right." Devona turned and left the room, shutting the door behind her.

Keuri waited a moment and then turned to Elainea. "I have something for you." Reaching into a worn bag that rested beneath the table, Keuri drew a set of clothing made from deer hide. It had been oiled and worked until it fairly shone in the flickering candle light. "In the south, all our women are given a set of battle garments once their training has ended. Though I know you will need all the finery and manners Devona can teach you if you are to be queen, for now, this will suit you far better in battle."

Elainea ran her fingers along the soft skins in awe, the stitches were so fine and the craftsmanship shone through in each piece. Lifting the britches she saw they would fit her quite snugly and the vest would go over the fresh white shirt folded at the bottom of the pile. Keuri tilted her chin towards the floor where a new pair of boots lay. Tears welled in Elainea's eyes as she brought the gift close to her chest. "I don't know what to say. Thank you does not seem adequate."

Kueri nodded and stood to leave. "You have earned these many times over. They will be much more comfortable than the split skirts you fashioned for yourself." Keuri winked as she shut the door behind her. Standing outside she inhaled the brisk air before turning towards her tent, oblivious to the slight movement in the shadows.

Chapter 11

SYBELLA WATCHED THE MORNING DAWN clear as the sun filtered through the early morning flurries that had blanketed the courtyard in white, offering a temporary cleansing of the charred remains of the town just beyond the gates. She clenched her jaw as another wave of pain passed over her. Jacob sat in the corner on his cot watching her closely. Her time had come, and with it another set of problems.

"Jacob, go and fetch Tabitha from the kitchen. I will need her today." Sybella instructed the boy without turning from the window. Jacob had proven himself loyal, doing as she bid with watchful eyes but no questions.

Sybella paced back and forth as she waited for him to return, rubbing her back with each pain that struck her body. Hearing footsteps stop outside her door she hurried to open it, and instantly regretted doing so.

"Sybella, I need you to perform a spell for me." David said with a smile that did not come close to lighting his obsidian eyes. Glancing down at her belly one eyebrow rose in disgust. "Or are you otherwise engaged?"

"No I am not, my Lord. I am only a bit tired as you can imagine." Sybella felt sweat building on her top lip as another wave of pain started in her back and wrapped around her belly. "Can Chumbra assist you with this task?"

"Chumbra is... away at the moment." David smirked. "However, I think it can wait a day or two until you are feeling rested."

"Thank you, my Lord. You are gracious as always." Sybella dipped her head and paused mid bow as she felt liquid trickling down her leg. Stepping quickly into the room she tried to shut the door, but David placed his foot stopping her.

"Sybella, remember our agreement. I will visit you again this afternoon and see that the child is properly discarded." David's sneer marred his face.

"Yes, my Lord. As you wish." Sybella mumbled without glancing up. The foot disappeared from the crack of the door. She managed to shut it before doubling over in pain. Hobbling over to the chair she leaned against it for a few moments until it passed. Jacob entered the room with Tabitha.

"Took you long enough brat!" she shouted in anger, if he had been here David would not have had to speak to her directly and would not have seen her situation, thereby giving her more time. Now she would have to rush, and rushing made things sloppy.

Jacob scowled at her turned back. "Apologies, Mistress. Tabitha is the same as you and can't walk very quickly."

"Do not make excuses, you sniveling ingrate! Get out! I no longer need you." Sybella flung her hands towards the door, dismissing the boy.

"Yes mistress." He eyed Tabitha who stood trembling in the center of the room, they had walked as quickly as she could manage and she was still out of breath. Catching her eye he nodded briefly, tilting his head towards the door and she smiled quickly in understanding. He would wait for her in the hallway.

Sybella took a moment to compose herself, then stood at the small table as she mixed various leaves into a pot of hot water. "Tabitha, please sit down. I know exactly how tired you must be right now. Are your ankles swollen as well? Mine are horrendous!"

"Umm thank you miss, and yes, I am a bit uncomfortable. But it is not proper for me to sit with you." Tabitha wrung her hands nervously beneath her apron that lay taut across her own swollen belly, ill at ease with the sudden switch in temperament of the woman before her.

"Nonsense, we women must come together in these times. Put stations aside for the moment and have tea with me." Sybella indicated a chair and watched the indecision play across the girl's features as she tentatively lowered her large body into it. "Now isn't that better dear?"

"Yes miss. 'Tis" Tabitha responded.

"Is this your first babe?" Sybella asked as she offered the other woman a cup of tea.

"No, this is my third. I have a girl of twelve and a boy of six; they stay with my mother while I work here." Tabitha answered as she held the cup in shaky hands.

"Don't be shy. The tea is a brew I mix to help ease the pains this pregnancy has brought on. It is my first, you see, and I was wondering if you could explain what I should expect in childbirth." Sybella said softly, glancing down into her own mug before taking a small sip.

"Oh, of course miss. Ain't nothing to be scared of at all! Our bodies are designed for this ya know. Just let things happen as they will, and your body will do the rest." Tabitha relaxed her shoulders, taking a large sip of tea. "Yes, miss. Nothin' to it at all. This tea has a peculiar taste to it. What did you say it was for?"

Sybella watched Tabitha as she began to shift uncomfortably in the chair. "Oh, a little of this, a little of that. It is an acquired taste, but really works to ease the pain. Drink up." Sybella watched as Tabitha drained the last of the tea and set the cup down before she squinted in discomfort and rubbed the side of her belly.

"Well, it looks like my time maybe sooner than I thought miss." Tabitha grunted as a sudden pain took over. "I better get back to me rooms, miss."

"Nonsense Tabitha, you are right where you are meant to be. What better way to learn of childbirth than to see it firsthand." Sybella finished drinking her own cup of tea and leaned into the ensuing wave of pain.

Sybella muttered a few words activating the spell she had cast over the room, preventing any sounds from escaping into the hall. Standing, Sybella roughly shoved Tabitha from the chair and onto the floor.

"Miss please, please. Ohhhhh, I need help miss. The babe is coming!" Tabitha moaned, writhing in pain.

"Yes, yes. Both our babies are coming, but you need not concern yourself with that now. Just push." Sybella watched as Tabitha gritted her teeth and bore down with each wave of pain. She eyed the rush of blood and water that gushed out from between the woman's bent knees. She listened with apathy to the screams of pain as the child slipped from the woman onto the cold floor and made no sound.

"Uggghh!!! The Baby! Miss, please wrap my baby! Is it a boy or girl?" Tabitha panted and tried to lift herself from the floor to see, but Sybella had scooped the child up after roughly cutting the cord and turned her back on the woman.

"I am sorry Tabitha, your baby did not live." Sybella said as she tightly wrapped a cloth around the wiggling infant. Clutching it to her chest as another pain signaled her own child about to enter the world.

"Noooooo! YOU LIE!" Tabitha wailed. "Someone help me! The witch has killed my baby! Help me please!"

"No one can hear you woman!" Sybella said as she grunted, lying on her back she bore down as she had seen Tabitha do.

Straining with the pain wracking her body she cast the now still infant aside as she felt her body seemingly ripped in two. Screaming she pushed one last time and felt a small body slither from beneath her dress into her waiting hands. Panting she lifted it to her chest and marveled at the sight before her. A wrinkly little girl with a red mark just between her squished eyes wailed in her arms. Wrapping the baby in her shawl she gently placed her on a fur before cutting the cord that had tied them together for the last few months.

Glancing over at Tabitha she was relieved to see the unmoving chest and glassy eyes staring vacantly out of the window, the setting sun reflecting in the blood pooled around her lower body. *This would make things a little easier*, Sybella thought as she pushed sweaty hair out of her face. Limping over to her chest she retrieved a vial and collected some of the spilled blood, there were few things as powerful as the shed blood of an innocent. Standing over the dead woman Sybella placed her own afterbirth on Tabitha's significantly smaller belly while she began to sway and chant. Clapping her hands once released a spark that ignited the blood and body in a blaze that burned so swiftly and so hot that only ash was left behind. With a few more words a breeze lifted the gray pile into the air and out the open window. Once she was sure no trace of the woman remained, she removed the spell from the room and called for Jacob.

"Yes mistress." Jacob answered, looking around the room for Tabitha but not seeing her. Instead, he caught a faint scent of copper that caused his stomach to turn and two wrapped bundles, one that moved slightly and one that did not. Looking to Sybella, the color drained from his face as he realized she had given birth. He remembered the screams as his mother had brought his little sister in the world, the only explanation for the missing woman and the silent birth was magic, dark magic.

"I need you to take this baby and leave the manor. Go wherever you like, only guard her with your life. If anything happens to her, I will find you and kill you very slowly. Do you understand?" Sybella brought the child towards him.

"Yes, mistress." Jacob uttered, too shocked to say anything else.

"Tell no one of this. Of ANY of this." Sybella threatened him.

"Y-yes, mistress," Jacob whimpered.

Sybella took a moment to gaze into the eyes of the child she would never know, and placed a kiss on the mark. "Make sure she is happy."

Jacob almost didn't hear the soft words, but the look on Sybella's face would stay with him for as long as he lived. No matter the evil that flowed through her veins, in this moment she was a mother and he saw her pain.

"What is her name, mistress?" Jacob asked.

She shoved the child into his arms. "You name her. She is yours now." Sybella pushed the two of them towards the door. "Wait." Biting her lip she surveyed the room and wondered if there was anything she could give the child, something of worth that could be sold or at least be held as a reminder that for a moment, she had been loved. Her eyes ceased their roaming and focused on her trembling hands, slipping the serpentine ring from her finger she uttered a spell that removed the poison from it. The curse tying it to Ashrek had been broken, it would serve a better purpose now. "Take this; give it to her when she is old enough to understand." Squeezing Jacob's fingertips around the ring she pushed them out of the room, closing the door gently. Leaning against the barrier that separated her from her daughter she listened to hasty footsteps as Jacob whisked her child away forever. Pressing her teeth into her bottom lip until it drew blood she allowed a few tears to fall. She had to remind herself that she had never wanted children, that she was strong and love was a weakness exploited by the strong or a crutch for the weak. Straightening her back she cleaned herself up quickly, gathered the dead infant and left to meet with the king.

Chapter 12

ASHREK GRIMLY WATCHED THE SUN SET on yet another day of inaction from his generals. They sat around the table drinking more than they strategized and he had had enough of the delay. Looking at the faces of the men he had selected based solely on the advice of his father - his dead father, he could not help but wonder if the guidance had been intentionally misleading. None of the men here had seen a day of battle; they were all just as inexperienced as he. His father had kept the older and therefore wiser men for his own army. Ashrek's remaining eye narrowed in anger, he was done with this charade!

"Who among you has fought in battle?" He said, but they were so deep in their cups no one responded. "WHO AMONG YOU HAS FOUGHT IN BATTLE!" He yelled and slammed his fist against the table causing the cups to spill some of their contents. Still no one answered. They merely looked down in shame, not seeing the slight twitch of his fingers. Suddenly, they began to cough and wheeze, eyes bleeding and hands clawing at throats. A vein in Ashrek's forehead pulsed as he released his power against the weak men sitting around him. One by one they collapsed across the table or onto the floor as they tried in vain to escape his grasp. He stopped the flow of blood in their veins and killed them as painfully and as slowly as he could. When the room was deathly silent he called for his attendant.

"Clean this mess up and issue a summons to the men of Arcana. I need generals." Ashrek stalked past the trembling ashen-faced man. "Have them appear before me in two days. We march in one week."

"Yes sir." The man said, barely able to breathe over the scent of bodily fluids and death in the dining hall. Ashrek seethed the entire way back to his room, why had it taken him so long to realize the sabotage his father had initiated. He had never wanted him to succeed in ruling, had in fact planned to have him come crawling back for help when battle proved imminent. *Crack!* The wood framing his door split where his fist made impact, ignoring the blood dripping from his knuckles he paced and finally settled before the fire that blazed. Snow was falling heavily outside and they would need to travel quickly, if they had any hopes of reaching Nuru Manor. The mountain pass would be blocked soon. Traveling by sea would be just as treacherous. The winter sea had claimed dozens of ships over the years, travel by land would take longer but would ensure more soldiers lived long enough to die on the battlefield. They could wait no longer, it was time to move.

Ashrek let his shoulders droop in exhaustion, wincing at the throbbing ache in his hand that echoed the pulsing behind his missing eye. Retiring, he drew the heavy drapes closed around his bed and lay down; in a moment he was dreaming of the clash of swords and revenge.

Dawn came quickly, and with it the sound of voices and rushing feet in the corridor. Flinging his shirt on and stepping into his britches he ripped the door open. "What is going on?" He shouted, watching several servants flinch away from his wrath.

"Apologies sir, but there is a group gathered in the courtyard. We are trying to disperse them, but they are adamant in wishing to speak with you."

Ashrek slammed the door in the servant's face and dressed quickly, was it possible the call for men and generals had caused this much of a response? He hoped the men he found would be trained, ready and thirsty for blood. They had precious little time to wait. Outside, he drew his cloak close against the cold air. His jaw went slack as he looked on those before him. A cluster of women stood armed from top to bottom for war.

"Ha ha ha! You cannot be serious!" Ashrek wiped the tears from his eyes before they could freeze in the wind. "I called for MEN and this is the response I get? No offense ladies...no, yes take offense please. Unless you are here to warm my bed, be gone. I need generals not ladies' maids." Ashrek dismissively turned his back on them only to stop in his tracks as he felt the whisper from an arrow graze his cheek and lodge in the door before him at eye level, the THWAP of it echoing in the crisp morning air. Turning back he eyed the women again. "Perhaps I misjudged you. Who are you?"

A woman stepped forward. She was tall and cloaked in a black wolf skin. Her dark eyes peered at him from behind the fanged skull of the animal. White paint streaked down the bridge of her nose and across both cheeks. The skin that he could see was dark and contrasted sharply with white teeth when she spoke with a heavily accented but strong voice. "We are the lifeblood of Arcana, the guardians of the temple and the defenders of the faith. We are Nitralii."

Each warrior lifted her left foot and slammed it down in unison as their leader's words rippled through the air. He had heard of this faction of warrior women, though he had thought them nothing more than myth. Strapped to each back was a staff with wicked curved blades on both ends and a shield painted black with stripes that mirrored the war paint on their faces. Braces of fur and leather covered their forearms and thick boots laced up their legs over britches of varying shades of black and gray. He imagined they could melt into shadows and dark nights seamlessly and attack with deadly precision.

"Why have you answered the call for war? I have no faith in your Dark Lord. I have killed many of your fellow believers and razed the temple to the ground. Why should I trust you to lead my army against the very one you worship?" Ashrek crossed his arms and gazed at the woman.

"What you say is true, you should not trust us. We could just as easily have slit your throat as you lay sleeping behind dark curtains, as we could have with the arrow through your skull a moment ago. We chose not to do either." The woman smirked seeing Ashrek's eyes widen a fraction. "We will lead your army against the one who claims to fight for the light. After he is defeated, we will return to our land and you will be on your own against our master."

"What is your name?" Ashrek growled.

"You may call me Lenara," she responded.

"*Lenara*, how will I know that you will not just turn on me in the middle of battle? Defect to David's side like your black hearted mistress?"

"You do not. But know this," Lenara took a step forward. "We are here at the request of our lord. Whom you disrespectfully refer to as 'David'. He has advised us through visions that we are to aid you in this and ONLY this. Our allegiance is absolute and how he chooses to kill you, because he will, is entirely at his pleasure. We will find your men and begin training them. We will be ready to march within a week." Lenara turned on her heel and walked towards the barracks, the other four women fell in step behind her without saying a single word.

Ashrek clenched his jaw in frustration. That they would have the gall to take command and dismiss him so carelessly spoke volumes about what they truly thought of him. The servants averted their eyes and hurried to their assigned tasks, careful to appear oblivious to the disrespect they had just witnessed. Ashrek was still a very dangerous and sometimes erratic man, it was always best to stay out of the path of his ire.

"Mother, are you sure this is the path we are meant to take? Assisting the blasphemers?" Serena asked as they made their way towards the barracks.

Lenara looked at the youngest member of the warriors under her control, she understood the fear and uncertainty the girl was feeling. This would be her first foray into battle, first time defending the clan and the Dark Lord. She would be forced to put her honor, her very life on the line for what she claimed to believe, it was only natural she had questions. Natural, but also highly disrespectful.

"I will allow this lapse in obedience only this once daughter. You serve the Dark Lord and I am his voice, while that is true you will do what I say when I say it." Lenara's eyes softened seeing the girl's downcast eyes. "I understand Serena, I was afraid during my first battle as well. Have faith in the one you follow, he is a vengeful lord and will bring a swift end to those who have desecrated his sacred temples, killed his followers, and turned so many astray. We will be on the side of victory and your name will echo in the halls of time!"

Lenara watched as the downcast eyes lifted to meet hers with pride and determination, shifting, they touched foreheads before stepping inside the barracks.

Jacob had managed to convince the cook to allow him to sleep in the storage room, claiming Sybella had cast him aside. He stared into the face of the infant sleeping in an empty crate and wrapped in a burlap sack. He was ashamed that the scratchy fabric had to be placed on her delicate skin but it was the best he could do. He remembered the soft clothes his mother had wrapped his sister in and sighed. He had to come up with a name for the child, his sister's name instantly came to mind but was quickly cast aside, it wouldn't be right. This child was the spawn of evil and didn't deserve...

The child opened her eyes and stared silently as if hearing his thoughts. Her eyes were a peculiar mix of colors, like the pearls his mother collected when they last visited the Draken sea, one moment they appeared gray and then changed to purple with a pinkish hue. As he stared he felt as if he was falling into their swirling depths, his jaw became slack and he could have sworn he heard a soft voice whisper something he couldn't quite make out. Then she blinked, breaking the connection. Rubbing his forehead he looked at the baby from the side of his eye, yeah something was off with her. A memory fluttered at the edges of this mind pricking his eyes with tears he swore never to shed. Jacob could almost feel the caress of his mother's fingertips, soft as rose petals, as she brushed the tears from his cheeks.

"It's not fair!" Jacob said, "she's just a baby! Why is she chosen and I am not?"

"You are chosen my love. Both of you are." She whispered into his dark coiled hair, squeezing him closer to her chest. She understood his confusion and feelings of rejection. Jacob wrapped one of his fingers in the dark coils that flowed over her shoulder.

"Then why can't I do what she can? Why is she better than me?" Jacob grumbled as he wiped his runny nose on a sleeve.

"I'll tell you what my mother told me, what her mother told her and what every mother tells her child. You are special, you are loved by The One. He has gifted all those who follow the way of light and even those who do not. Each gift is unique, some are more obvious than others, like your sister. She can move things with her mind, remember when she knocked over the milk?" She said, meeting his gaze with her own amber one.

"Ha ha! Yes that was funny! She cried though, that part wasn't funny." Jacob said.

"Yes, well she doesn't understand what she is capable of yet and may one day wish she were gifted like you are."

"Me? I'm nothing special mama." Jacob said, looking down.

"Oh yes you are! You are a natural learner! You have taken to reading and writing and doing your sums better than even your FATHER!" She leaned in closer, "I'll tell you a secret, but you must promise not to let on that you know. Promise?" She waited until he nodded enthusiastically. "Alright. Your father has had to confer with the village elders for books of greater difficulty for you! The

94

ones you are now reading are the oldest texts available, even your father can not understand them. But YOU can!"

She grinned as she watched the light flood his eyes, pride filling his small chest.

"Some people can speak to animals, some can work with their hands and make the earth yield a harvest no matter the season. Some can control the elements while others can heal. I have even heard of those that can mesmerize others with a glance or a voice so pure it causes all to obey. There are so many different talents in the world, you must never compare yourself to anyone Jacob. You were created as you are for a purpose, a reason only The One knows. You must seek him, follow the way of light and your destiny will reveal itself in time."

"Mother what is your gift?"

"You don't know? Maybe I haven't been doing a good job of using it. It's Love! I can love you and our family and even our enemies. Love is the greatest gift of all." She said with a wink before rubbing her nose against his.

"You're right! Your love is the best gift ever!"

Jacob remembered that hug; it was the last one he had received from her. His parents had done a good job at keeping the darkness outside from entering their home, until that day. The day they were ripped from him and he was forced into the very shadow of the beast. He stared into the relaxed face of the sleeping infant and knew she was gifted. Her mother would not have told her about the way of light nor of how The One loved her, chose her, but he could. His mother had said The One listened and spoke to those who believed.

"If you are listening like my mother said you are, what should I name this baby?" After a few moments he felt a stirring in his chest and a sweet fragrance surrounded him, a voice that he could barely hear whispered, *Renee.*

Jacob smiled down at the child who had opened her strangely colored eyes. "Renee, yeah, that's pretty. Any thoughts on how we get out of the manor Ren?"

Chapter 13

THE SHADOWS PLAYED ACROSS THE SCARRED features of Akronius as he stood guard with Nguvu and the pack. Clouds passed over the face of the moon momentarily casting them all in darkness before shifting once again and illuminating the encampment in its silver glow. The ears of the Dire Wolves swiveled and muscles twitched as movement beside one of the tents caught their attention. Taking one step towards the motion Akronius saw a slim figure slip out and dart towards the river.

Tapping into his gift Akronius channeled the stealth of the Dire Wolves, eyes glowing burnished gold as he crept behind the person. Whoever it was, they were skilled. Their feet moved swiftly and silently, stepping around anything that might announce their presence to the sleeping masses around them. The figure paused at the edge of the ice covered river. Akronius saw the glint of the moon flash across the blade held in the small hands.

"Reveal yourself!" Akronius shouted as he extended his hand into talons as deadly as Syphras.

"You always were good at staying in the shadows Akronius." The feminine voice replied, though she did not move from her position.

"Devona. What are you doing creeping around in the middle of the night?" Akronius asked, his hand returning to normal and resting on the sword at his side.

"I ran out of water. I thought it would be easier to collect some of this ice and heat over a fire rather than begging one of you to carry a bucket for me. I am no fool. I know where I stand here. It is best I stay out of sight as much as possible. Don't you agree?" The thwack of her blade echoed softly into the night, as she chipped away at the frozen river. Standing, she turned revealing hands wrapped in her black cloak to shield them from the cold of the ice chunk she held.

Akronius watched as she walked towards him, she had put on a few pounds and almost resembled the Devona he knew in the past, almost. She was missing the arrogance and the malevolence that had lit her eyes, a reflection of her dark soul. Since she had arrived in the camp she had in fact kept to herself, after every offer to help was refused and every request for assistance was met with steely glares. She was not trusted and rightfully so.

"Can you really blame anyone other than yourself for that?" He inquired, wondering if she really thought it would be so easy to insert herself into their plans.

"Well, I had hoped." She responded softly, stopping to the side of him, watching the woods blink with glowing eyes here and there. "You made it seem so easy. How did you do it? You, who has so much blood on his hands, and darkness within that rivals mine. How did you fool everyone into welcoming you with open arms?"

She had been trying to fit in, and Akronius heard the bitterness in her words. "It was not easy and I did not fool, or even try to fool anyone. I was changed slowly and over time by…" he hesitated.

"By what?" Devona hissed, turning to face him fully. The hatred in her face became clear in the twilight.

Akronius felt pity flood his heart as he saw his old self reflected in her eyes. "Love. Unconditional love, from someone who had nothing to gain and everything to lose. You could find this peace as well, but it will take time. You have to be willing to accept the course and the consequences."

"Ha!" Devona laughed. "You think you're so much better than me, don't you? Well let me remind you, YOU ARE NOT!" The frigid air created puffs of breath with every word as she stepped closer to him, the dagger still visible at her waist. "I know who you are, Akronius. Even if you try to forget and everyone thinks you have changed. I know the blood that stains your hands. I know the innocent lives that have been cut short by your blade. I know the thrill you felt as you watched the light dim in your victim's eyes and the joy at taking their belongings as your own. I remember how excited their screams and pleading cries for mercy made you. That man is still there, just like those scars on your face. He will always be there, waiting."

Akronius smirked as her face shifted from gloating to uncertainty and then fear. Her eyes widening a fraction as a low growl rumbled just behind her from an outcropping of rocks, her hand lowered to her side, he stepped forward, whispering into her ear. "Think what you will Devona. Time will tell which of us is on the right path."

She watched him walk towards the rocks and stifled a gasp as two slanted eyes stared back at her from the blue tinted boulders. Scales rippled across its surface and she had to crane her head back as she came face to face with his familiar.

Syphra bared her teeth letting a drop of acid fall and scorch the earth, the snow melting on impact. *Should I kill her?* Syphra whispered across their connection.

"Devona, this is Syphra. You were heading back to your tent, right?" Akronius watched the woman pale and clutch the ice closer to her chest.

"Y-yes, I was just leaving, good night Akronius. Syphra." Devona walked quickly back to her tent, stumbling over her feet in her haste.

She is not truthful, I can sense deep darkness in her. Syphra said. Her azure eyes appraising the man standing beside her.

"I know Syphra. I know who she is and who she is pretending to be. We will keep a watchful eye on her." Akronius agreed as he caressed the elegantly scaled neck.

And she is wrong, you are not who you used to be. Syphra lowered her neck until she could press her forehead against his. *Your past shapes you, but it does not define you. Your choices have led you to redemption and rebirth. Do not let the small-minded thoughts of others cause you to doubt who you are in the present.*

Thank you my friend. Akronius whispered back to her mind, their mutual respect flowed over their bond deepening their connection. Together they watched the sky change from inky darkness to dustings of pink and orange as the sun brought on a new day from the east.

Chapter 14

THE DARK LORD WATCHED AS SYBELLA entered his chamber. She walked slowly clearly in pain, but held her head high. Dipping into a curtsy she lifted a bundle in trembling hands. "My Lord, I have done as you demanded. The child is no longer an issue."

David lifted an eyebrow in surprise. "You did this yourself?"

"I thought it best to rectify the problem myself, since I created it to begin with. You need not concern yourself with such lowly tasks when there are far greater things you are meant to be doing." Sybella said, standing proudly she kept her eyes lowered.

David watched her, she did not fidget and when she raised her eyes she held his gaze unwaveringly. "Very well. The task I have for you will require expertise."

Sybella smirked, "I am sure Chumbra took his inadequacy well."

David tilted his head, "Chumbra has served his ultimate purpose and received his reward."

Sybella felt the blood drain from her face as realization set in, Chumbra was dead.

She watched the smile bloom across David's face as he saw understanding dawn in her eyes. "Are we all to receive this reward, my Lord?" Sybella asked.

"Time will tell, my child. Time Will Tell. For now I need a shadow warrior spell. I trust your books have the necessary information and ingredients to cast this?"

"Yes my lord, I'll get started on it immediately." Sybella drew the baby's stiffening body to herself and turned to leave the room.

"Leave the child." David said, though he whispered it, the stiffening of her shoulders indicated she had heard him. "The table there will do."

Sybella looked to her left at the small wooden table and placed the bundle gently down, her hand lingered on the still baby. Nothing else sat on the table, it was alone. Straightening she headed once more for the door, glancing back in time to see a single shaft of light break through the clouds and surround the baby. Feeling the eyes of David on her, she hurried from the room, ignoring the tingle of doubt in her chest. The echoes of her steps in the empty hallway rang loudly in her ears, the manor employed very few willing to serve under the Dark Lord and the emptiness felt as if it were closing in on her.

Reaching her quarters Sybella leaned against the closed door, heart racing she could still feel the burn from David's eyes on her back. Looking at the clean and empty room, she felt her resolve slipping. The indention from her daughter's small body was still visible in the fur rug near the fireplace. She wrapped one hand around the doorknob pressing into the small of her back and then released her grip. No, it was better this way. Determined, she walked to the table and her spell books. It did not take long to find the one he wanted, *Shadow Warriors*. It was a relatively easy incantation and she had an idea on whom he would unleash them. She had heard the whispers of the army gathering near the Spyre River, if it could be called an army. Spies reported a mere thousand troops consisting of old men and women. The power of her master would sweep through their numbers like a warm knife through pig fat.

Time was marked only by the shadows creeping across the room as she focused intently on measuring each ingredient, adding it to her mortar and crushing them together with the bone pestle. When she was ready she gathered the bowl and headed back to her master's chamber, her knuckles had not made contact with the wooden door when she heard, "Enter."

"It is ready my lord. I only need one more ingredient." Sybella said meeting the obsidian gaze of David.

"If you need more, then you are not ready." He replied

"No, my Lord. You misunderstand me. I do not need anything, YOU need to add your essence to activate it." Sybella corrected.

"Ah. Very well, come. Your timing is perfect." David said gesturing to the setting sun through the window.

Sybella set the bowl on the table where the infant had been only a few hours ago. Flicking her eyes around the room she saw no sign of it, but she caught David watching her and refocused on the task at hand. Drawing a blade from her cloak she sat it next to the bowl and stepped away.

"You will need to add your blood to this and then recite the incantation. I can write it down if you…"

"No need. I know it." David cut her off. Lifting the blade he cut a line across the center of his palm and squeezed several drops of thick black blood into the bowl. It immediately began to smoke and swirl together as he started speaking over it.

"Fire and Ash, blood and bone. From my essence you will roam. Shadow to shadow, leap and bound. Corporeal to incorporeal with death surround. From this curse none can flee, sunlight alone can vanquish thee. Reach out and crush, destroy the heart. Amorphous Noctem Volant." As he shouted the last word a ring of darkness rushed from the center of the bowl and out beyond the manor walls into the night.

Kaison stood guard at the edge of the forest, something was wrong. The wolves paced and growled and his own heart felt heavy, his shoulders tense but in preparation for what he did not know. It was quiet, too quiet, his eyes scanned the shadowed tree limbs for a danger he could only feel.

"Show yourself," he demanded. "I know you're out there." Placing his left hand on the hilt of his sword he braced for whatever would come. Instead he was shoved onto his heels by a strong gust of freezing wind. It whipped his cloak, stole his breath and brought stinging tears to his eyes. Rushing to brace against a nearby tree he watched in horror as the wind rushed through the branches spitting hundreds of rapidly moving creatures from the gloom, specters that leapt from tent to tent, diving into the darkness and emerging from shadows. One brushed against a nearby wolf and it dropped instantly, shocked blue eyes locked with his then faded to vacancy in death. Kaison watched as the specters seemed to melt into the shadowed tents and imagined the bodies of his comrades falling victim in the same manner.

"SHAMA!" Kaison bellowed into the night, and it took barely a moment for the man to emerge. Wide eyed, he took in the situation, horror flashed rapidly across his face before quickly being replaced by determination as he grasped the staff that never left his side in both hands and closed his eyes.

"HEAR ME YOU SPIRIT OF DESTRUCTION! YOU ARE NOT WELCOME IN THIS CAMP! I rebuke you in the name of The One. The One who brings to light all things done in the dark. The One who speaks and restores life. The One who was, is and will always be! The One and ONLY ruler of this plane of existence, The Destroyer of Darkness! Be Gone!" Striking his staff into the earth the etching on his staff began to glow brighter and brighter until it resembled daylight and Kaison had to shield his eyes. The light found every shadow and illuminated it. There was no place for the creatures to hide. Some tried unsuccessfully to reach the forest but the light was faster, it penetrated every creature and tore them apart. Shama lowered his arms and exhaled, meeting Kaison's eyes then shifting to allow Alric to exit the home closely followed by Elainea.

"This is why I insisted you sleep in the house; protections have been put in place for your safety," Shama whispered. "We can take no chances with your lives."

Tears glazed the eyes of Elainea as the first slit of dawn breached the mountains and the wailing reached her ears. She could not grasp how her life could be of more value than any other, of the thousand men and women who had rallied to their side, 400 had lost their lives. Snuffed out like candles in the wind. The weight of their sacrifice settled heavily on her shoulders as she and the generals walked through the people. Assessing the carnage they offered words of encouragement, an understanding hand on a trembling shoulder, an embrace for the grief stricken, but it was not enough. It would never be enough.

As the sun rose higher in the sky, the thick blanket of snow was cleared from one area and several pyres were erected. Alric and Elainea stood together watching the greatly diminished army stand stooped and defeated, red rimmed eyes looking at them, some pleading for answers and others for revenge.

Elainea looked to her brother who nodded and whispered a few words to Eret. The crowd took several steps back as the earth heaved beneath the feet of the red haired woman before them, lifting her above their heads.

"I stand here grieving with you. Grieving FOR you and those you... WE have lost this day. This was a cowardly attack carried out by one who fears what we stand for. Yet I stand here to tell you NOT to forget this feeling. This pain. FEEL IT, all of it and use it. Let the emotions rise to the surface and stay there. And know that the one we fight for feels your pain too. He feels your anguish. He stands with us! He will not abandon us now so do not abandon Him. Our land, our families are broken and we cannot fix them on our own. Raise your heads and hold them high! Look to the light, to The One who will fight for us! WITH US! Every tear that falls He will catch, every innocent life that has been stolen He will avenge. We are not weak. We are not powerless. We are not without HOPE! The One will pour His strength into each of us and we will fight! We will fight and WE. WILL. WIN!" Stretching her hand out, Elainea sent tongues of flames arching through the air to light the dozens of pyres as a deafening roar erupted from the crowd while the earth trembled beneath the stamping of booted feet. One by one each person returned to their tents and began preparations for the long march to the battlefield, leaving Alric and Elainea alone watching the flames rise and the ashes fall, turning the white snow gray.

"That is why you were chosen Laney. You are the spark The One will use to purify this land." Alric said softly.

108

"I suppose so." Elainea replied, wiping a tear from her windblown cheek. Sighing deeply she looked around. "Now how do we get down from here?"

Chapter 15

JACOB PRAYED FERVENTLY THAT REN would stay asleep until he returned; it was a prayer he had repeated multiple times over the last few days. Escaping was taking far longer than he had expected. Someone was always giving him a task to do and no matter where he went it was as if he could feel eyes on him. Every time he passed Sybella in the halls she had looked through him, never acknowledging him and never asking about the child, how could a mother be so cruel? *Renee is definitely better off with me*, he thought.

"Boy, Sybella is looking for you." The cook said to him one morning. It had been 3 days since the child was born and it was getting harder to keep her silent. He kept her wrapped tightly and hidden in a crate deep in the storage room where he slept, visiting several times a day to feed and change her clothes. It was remarkable they had lasted this long without discovery, and that knowledge only served to affirm how *different* she was from other babies.

"You better get a move on boy!" The cook flicked a rag at him as he rushed out into the hall, heading for the room he had done everything to avoid. After knocking lightly he entered the room. "You called for me mistress?"

Sybella did not glance up from the book she was reading. "I need you to go into the wood and collect a special mushroom. It is very rare and deadly if handled incorrectly. It will be used to coat the tips of the arrows of our army, we march in two days' time so I need you to fill this bag with them, do not bother returning if you fail me in this." She shook an empty sack at him, their fingers touched and she squeezed them slightly, that was all he needed. She had given him a window and he would take it.

Running down the hall he skidded into the kitchen with the sack clutched in his hand. "Uh--I have to --Uh go out! Sybella needs me to gather some ingredients, may I take some milk and bread with me? Please?" Jacob rushed to add, "I don't want to keep her waiting."

"Take whatever you need boy," the cook said. "And take one of these bottles as well, milk soaked cloth is not the way to feed a babe."

Jacob looked at the cook in shock. "Did you really think you could hide a baby in MY kitchen and I not know? Be gone with ya." The cook's wink took the sting out of the rebuke. Jacob hurried to fill his sack and then using a long scrap of fabric strapped the tiny infant to his back and put on his cloak. With a final glance at the cook he left the warmth of the kitchen. "May the light protect ya both." he heard the cook whisper as he shut the door.

No one stopped him as he left the grounds of the manor, the guards only watched him silently as he walked through the gates. Feeling a tingle work its way up his neck he glanced back at the manor to see a shadow in the recesses of a window, it was there and gone so quickly it could have a reflection or his mind playing tricks on him. No, he knew who it was and as much as he despised her, he thanked her for the means to gain their freedom.

Ahead lay the charred remains of his hometown. He had no idea why the king had burned it to the ground weeks ago. Nor did he know if anyone had made it out alive. He walked over the brittle dirt road towards the woods. Nothing seemed to survive the darkness sweeping through the land. His only hope lay in reaching the Spyre River and the group of people gathering there.

Once he was sure no one else was around, he sat near a tree and unstrapped the baby from his back. She lay silently in his arms gazing up at him with those strange eyes that seem to draw him into their swirling depths. "Ren, we made it out! And I even have a real bottle for you now, isn't that something." Jacob poured some of the milk from his flask into the bottle and watched as she suckled greedily. "Yeah, much better than the cloth right. Sorry it took so long."

Looking around he judged it would take about a week to reach the river if he followed the road, but he only had enough milk for a day or two. Hopefully they would cross paths with a goat or a cow somewhere. And if not, snow melted and they could live on water for a while. Strapping her to his chest beneath the cloak, he patted her narrow back until she belched. "Thata girl," he whispered into her wispy black hair before continuing their journey. "Let's go find our own destiny."

Lenara stood to the side as the men sparred with each other under the watchful eye of her generals, in the two weeks since her arrival they were as ready as they were going to be. They had been more skilled than she had expected and only needed some additional direction. Though they would never match the skill of her group, *no one could be that good* she thought. Walking onto the field each general whistled sharply and the men formed ranks, a different whistle and the formation changed. *Perfect, they are ready,* she thought.

"Sir, there is something you must see." Ashrek looked up at the young man standing in the doorway.

"What is it?" He said impatiently.

"It's the men sir. They are... it's been hours... you have to see it." He was flustered and beckoned Ashrek to follow him.

Walking out into the dawn Ashrek felt his eyes widen, rows of men stood ready in full battle armor. No one spoke, no one moved, only the snap of the soldiers blood-red capes flapping in the wind broke the silence.

"We are ready to march. *My Lord.*" Lenara said from his left, the distaste for his position dripping from her lips.

"Get my armor." Ashrek said to the awestruck man who had summoned him. "We march at once."

"Another messenger has arrived from your nephew my lord. Will you see him or?" Bastien asked.

"Tell him what we have told all the others and send him on his way." Lord Alcherist dismissed the man without even a glance. His focus was solely on the gurgling child toddling across the fur rug and the smiling women reaching for him. His family was whole again, nothing could drag him from their presence ever again. As a bonus Bastien had proven to be intelligent as well as obedient, he had taken to the trivial issue of governing the people with ease, title meant nothing to the man. He only wanted what everyone wanted, for his family to be well taken care of and no threat of being shipped off to fight in a war he did not believe in. Easy terms to agree to, in exchange Alcherist became the voiceless face of an agnostic people.

Chapter 16

JACOB STUMBLED THROUGH THE FOREST, cold, hungry and wet. The milk from the goat he had found had run out the night before, and Renee had stopped crying a few hours ago. He had to find the army and fast. He should have reached the river by now. He was lost and dangerously close to giving up hope.

"Please, help us." He whispered, the words rising to the overcast sky on puffs of mist from wind chapped lips as he sank to his knees. Crawling to the base of a tree he drew the cloak tightly around them. "I'm sorry little one. I failed." He felt miserable as his eyes drifted closed.

They had been sitting in the shelter of the large tree roots for minutes or maybe hours when a wet nose pressed between the folds of his cloak, whining for his attention. Opening bleary eyes he came nose to nose with a large animal, blinking several times before the blue eyes came into focus followed by large ears and dense gray fur. *A wolf!* Jacob felt as if his eyes would pop from his head as he kept as still as possible, praying it would leave them alone, squeezing his eyes in disbelief, just as Renee took that very moment to begin wailing pitifully. The wolf startled, taking a step back before rushing off into the frost coated underbrush.

"Shush, shh. It's alright Ren, it's not safe here. We have to keep moving. I'm sorry, I know you're hungry." Removing the bottle filled with water from his waistband he tried to get her to drink, she thrashed her tiny head in refusal. Her cheeks grew redder and her crying became louder. Looking around in a panic he got up and hurried deeper into the woods. "Maybe it won't come back. Maybe we can find a farm nearby." Jacob talked to himself. A branch snapped behind him and he whipped around from one direction to another as more branches began to snap all around him. He began to run, one hand holding the miserable child to his chest and the other shielding his face from the barren branches and spindly needles of the trees surrounding him, only to smack into something so solid it knocked him onto his back. His vision swirled and a ringing began in his ears as a shadowy figure drew closer, leaning towards him.

"Mauuragg!" He tried to scream through the hand over his mouth.

"Hush boy!" The owner of the hand said roughly. "What are you doing out here alone and with a baby?"

Jacob's eyes popped open in shock as he realized it was a man and not a beast holding him down. "We are running from Nuru Manor sir. Me and my... sister, Renee."

"What is your name and where are you heading in the middle of winter?" The man asked.

"Jacob, sir. I heard of the army gathering by the river and hope to join them."

"Is that so?" The man pulled Jacob to his feet, brushing the snow from his cloak, peeking in at the child. "Sister huh? I'll take you back with me to the camp, and we'll sort everything out."

"C-c-camp?" Jacob stuttered, pulling back against the firm grip of the man. "Whose camp? Who are you?"

"My name is Kaison. You've been looking for us, seems we found you first. Come, we have healers and plenty of food for both of you. And don't mind the wolf."

Jacob let his body go slack in relief for only a moment. "WOLF!" His eyes grew wide as he finally noticed the same gray wolf standing nearby, its head cocked at an angle that would have been funny had it not been so terrifyingly large.

"Easy Jacob, easy. She is a friend, Naia found you and a good thing too. You wouldn't have lasted the night out here."

Jacob followed the man for a while, smelling the smoke from a campfire before he actually saw it. "Here we are." Kaison held the wooden door of the farmhouse open for Jacob to enter.

"Look what Naia found today." He announced to the group sitting around the table. Jacob felt his skin blanch under the scrutiny of so many.

"We were beginning to wonder where you had rushed off to," a red haired woman said, dropping the smile when she turned to him. "Are you a spy?"

Kaison chuckled. "Not many spies walking round in the dead of winter with a baby strapped to their chest Elainea."

"What!" She gasped.

Jacob opened his cloak, unwrapping the baby, holding her tightly as the woman, Elainea, stood and came closer. "My name is Jacob, and this is my sister Renee. I am no spy."

"Sister?" Elainea said with a raised brow, meeting the eyes of Kaison over Jacob's head, the baby's creamy complexion a stark contrast to the boy's brown skin. "Well siblings come in all forms I suppose. Where do you come from Jacob?"

"Nuru Manor." He said and watched as glances were exchanged around the table.

"Can I hold her? You both must be starving." Elainea asked as she reached for the silent baby, but Jacob took a step back preventing it. Elainea's eyes grew wide as she stared at the baby. "Shama, look at her eyes, have you ever seen a variation like this?"

Shama was silent as he stared into the small face of the baby girl. Her eyes were strange, but beautiful. "It is fortunate the two of you made it out of the manor Jacob. Your sister will be very strong. She will be gifted with persuasion, either with a look, a touch, her voice or all three. It is a very rare talent, one usually gifted to followers of the Dark Lord, and one not seen in many generations. If she had been left and found by David or The One forbid, Sybella…" Shama shuddered at the thought. "There is no telling what they would have forced her to do as she grew. You are safe with us. We will protect and train you both." Shama rubbed a fingertip down the downy soft cheek of the baby eliciting a smile that trapped him.

"Shama?" Alric said, and then repeated louder, placing a hand on the man's shoulder, "SHAMA?"

"Huh? Oh, oh dear." Shama shook his head and cleared his throat, stepping away from the baby. "Yes, powerful indeed."

Alric watched a white fog clear from his mentor's eyes. "I think it best if Jacob continues to tend to her needs. However unintentional, we cannot afford for any of us to fall under her spell. There is no telling what could happen."

"Where are your parents?" Kaison asked.

"Dead, sir. King David had them executed a few years ago as spies for Lord Vicrano. I have been a servant in the manor ever since." Jacob said.

"If that is true, how is this your sister?" Akronius said, leaning forward from where he sat at the table. "She isn't more than a week old."

Jacob swallowed and shrank back from the eyes staring at him. Taking a step towards the door he felt something solid behind him. Looking up over his shoulder his gaze locked onto the dark eyes of a bald man with scales, who flicked a forked tongue at him from behind sharp teeth.

"I...she..." Jacob stammered.

"Relax, Jacob." Keuri gently said, steering the boy towards a vacant chair at the table. "That is Zee, his bite is far worse than his bark. Just tell us why you are lying."

"I'm not." Jacob started and then stopped seeing the quirk of an eyebrow on Keuri's face. "She isn't my sister by blood. My baby sister was killed along with my parents. A woman in the manor begged me to take the baby with me when she found out I planned to run away. She promised not to give me away if I did it."

It was a half-truth that he hoped they would not see through.

"That wasn't so hard, right Jacob?" Keuri said, as she squeezed his arm and nodding in the direction of an old man sitting across from them. "Now, this is Lorox, he is blind but can see more than most and more importantly, can tell if you are still lying."

All eyes turned towards the old man and Jacob held his breath. "He is honest." The man said with a small smirk, everyone turned back to Jacob in relief.

"Good. You will stay with Alric and Shama for now. I assume you have a bottle for the babe?" Kaison said, taking the water filled bottle from Jacob, he emptied and refilled it with fresh milk. The room grew silent as they watched the tiny girl suckle greedily. One by one they walked out, Jacob casting a last look over his shoulder at Lorox who winked at him.

Jacob followed behind the large men and looked around in awe, everywhere he looked people were packing up. "Sir, where is everyone going?"

Alric looked down at the boy. "We are going to war, Jacob. We will be on the march by morning. It was fortunate that Naia found you when she did. Do you have anything else you want to tell us? About what is going on at the manor?" Alric clarified seeing the stricken look pass over the boy's brown face.

"Well, I overheard Sybella say something about poison arrows." Jacob said.

"That's good to know Jacob, we can take precautions now. Well done." Alric said with a smile. He felt a familiar nudging in his spirit and knew something was still off about what Jacob was telling them. He would wait and watch unless The One directed him further.

Chapter 17

ALRIC WATCHED THE LAST OF THEIR MEN walk around the bend in the road, their shadows blending into the gloom of the tree line in the setting sun. The wind blew coldly, ruffling the black hair brushing his shoulders. Drawing his cloak closer around himself he turned to face the mountain, his destiny would lead him to its craggy peaks in the coming days. Looking around at the farm where he had grown up, the snow covered earth had been trodden by hundreds of footsteps in every shape and size except for one small patch of ground near the frozen river. He was there before his mind realized his feet had moved.

"Mother, I hope you are at peace. I hope you are watching and looking over us with pride." The crunch of snow behind him drew his attention, but he continued. "We are afraid, mother. The battle is here, have we done what we were called to? What we were meant to do? Or did we miss an opportunity somewhere for peace. So many lives stand to be lost, I am not sure." Alric felt a gloved hand slip into his own.

"We are on the right path, Alric. Do not doubt The One now, we are almost there. Just like our men are waiting just out of sight, so is our victory. We cannot see it, but can't you FEEL it? I can." Elainea squeezed his hand. "I can feel it as I hold your hand. I can feel it in the breeze blowing down from the mountains. Darkness has held Elhaanai in its grip for long enough. Mother saw greatness in us, she believed in The One's destiny for us. It may not have turned out as she thought, as any of us thought, but it is the correct path. And the only way to the other side, the only way to reach daylight, is THROUGH the darkest night."

Elainea leaned her head against her brother's shoulder, they were not the children who had stood here so many years ago saying goodbye to their mother, beginning their journey. Now they were grown, preparing to face a battle for their lives and the lives of all who followed them. Looking across the frozen river Elainea whispered, "You came back from that forest different. Do not go back to the timid boy you were Alric. Be the man, the oracle, you are called to be and I will do the same as Queen. We will make our mothers proud."

Alric kissed his sister's red hair, a demonstration of affection the siblings rarely displayed. "Yes, my Queen." They walked off the farm, swords strapped at their sides, the spirit of their mothers hovering behind them.

The army marched through the night towards Nuru Manor, stopping when the sun began to rise. For six nights they marched and with the setting of the sun on the seventh day, the moon did not rise. The night was the blackest any of them had seen.

"We are here," Alric told the generals. "Have the men set up camp. The battle will take place here."

When the sun rose on the following day Alric's heart broke on hearing the report from their scouts. Following one of the men he was almost brought to his knees at the sight before them, in the distance the remains of the town surrounding Nuru Manor sat beneath a coating of fresh snow. Charred pieces of wood poked through the white blanket that sparkled in the early morning light. This is what they were fighting against, a blight that would reach out and destroy everything in its path.

"By The One," Akronius whispered. "How could he do this? All the people! What happened to all the people?"

"Most of them fled to Vimeo, sir. Hundreds have joined the Dark Lords' army. Any who could not decide..." the scout gestured sadly towards the burned out town.

"Despicable!" Kaison said with anger. He knew what this town had looked like under his reign, how it had flourished. How the streets and market had been filled with voices, the children that had played in the fields. How many of their bones now lay buried? How much blood cried out for vengeance from the soil? He dashed the tears from his cheek, turning towards the others standing with him.

"How will we proceed?"

"With caution," Keuri said gently. Kaison took a shaky breath but nodded. "Let's get back to camp; we need to prepare the people to fight."

The cold wind swirled the black cape worn by David, his golden hair flecked with snowflakes shone in the midday sun, his obsidian eyes roving across the lines of soldiers standing at attention before him. Sybella stood at his side, garbed in a blood-red hooded cape edged in black, her ebony hair flowing over one shoulder as she smiled in approval. The silence lingered as cold air whipped around growing in intensity.

"Today I will solidify my rule over the land of men. Today, you will soak the battle field in the blood of my enemies. You will be my hands and feet, you will do my bidding without wavering and without question. You have pledged your souls for my cause, and I will hold you to those oaths. The light followers have boldly walked onto our land, thinking to spread their lies of a benevolent and loving God. WE KNOW THE TRUTH! Only I, the Lord of Darkness can truly give you what you desire. What you really need. Only I can lead you down the road of enlightenment! Follow me into battle, claim glory for yourself! Take what should have been yours all along, and kill any who stand in your way! TO BATTLE!" As David cried, he raised his arms high above his head. Stormy clouds began rolling in, bringing large snowflakes and a mighty gust of wind.

"TO BATTLE!" His army responded, unfazed by the malevolent weather encroaching closer.

"To battle." Sybella whispered, hoping her child was far from the fray.

The wind whipped Elainea's red hair wildly across her face, as she sat on horseback before her army. She looked into the eyes of those closest to her and saw the determination she felt reflected in the different hues reflected back at her. Her brother and the generals sat on horses to her left and right. The howling of the wind caused a shiver to race down her spine and she sat up straighter in the saddle.

"Today we face the enemy that has stolen the peaceful dreams of those who live in this land. We face the darkness that seeks to snuff out the light we carry, to stop us from spreading that light into the far reaches of this land. Look to your left and to your right, that is your brother and your sister. By blood and by faith, fight for them, fight with them, protect each other. Those we face are like blind children, following the direction of one who cares not for their safety. Keep that in mind when you engage them. Whenever possible, disarm or disable rather than kill, but not at the cost of your own life. We know the truth. We follow the light, WE ARE THE LIGHT. A single candle can try to defy darkness, two candles even more so, but a thousand candles can illuminate the night! BE THE LIGHT! SHINE IN THE DARKNESS! Let this unholy wind fan

the flames of our faith! SPREAD THE LIGHT! To Battle!"
Elainea cried.

"SPREAD THE LIGHT! TO BATTLE!" The army cried out
over and over. The shouts reached into the clouds where Akronius
and Syprha hovered, sent on a mission known only to the generals.

Chapter 18

"I should be on the front lines! Syphra and I are of more use to you there then flying off in the opposite direction for something you're not even sure will aid us in the battle!" Akronius said.

"Akronius, I know you do not understand but this is what must be. Neither I nor The One have led you astray thus far, do not begin to doubt us now." Shama rebuked him softly.

"It is not that I doubt the validity of what you say, only that someone else should go." Akronius insisted, "Auni can fly just as…"

"He cannot. The height and the temperature would be too much for him." Shama countered.

"What about your eagle? Could you not call him back for this?" Akronius suggested, looking at the others for backup and receiving none.

"His purpose is to remain in the glade. Not on the field of battle." Shama sighed, "It must be you."

Akronius folded his arms, looking down in defeat.

"Tell us again why he must take the stone to the mountain. Maybe its purpose needs to be clarified more to give him some peace of mind," Kaison said.

"The stone that Alric took from King Vernis' sword is cursed, as you well know," Shama said nodding towards Alric, "yet it holds untapped power. The

One has revealed to me that if it can be purified and joined with my staff, in the right hands it can turn the tide of the coming battle. Where Vernis used the darkness in it, we will use the light. Where he tried and failed, succumbing to madness, we can succeed and stand firm."

"And to be purified it must be placed in the sacred pool in the Mnara Mountains." Alric stated.

"Correct." Shama confirmed, "Your task is not what you would have wanted, I understand that. The same could be said for Alric. Though he trained and is as ready as any other soldier, he will not be engaging in hand to hand combat either. The battle he must fight will be done on the spiritual plane, not against flesh and blood. We each have our roles to play, Akronius."

"So be it." Akronius grumbled, flipping the tent flap angrily on his way out to find Syphra.

Elainea watched the skies as Akronius and Syphra took off for the mountains, she knew he resented the task but she hoped he would come to appreciate the role he was playing in their victory. She had no doubt they would be victorious, she only worried the price they would pay in the process.

The army looked like a colony of ants far below as Akronius nudged Syphra towards the distant Mnara Mountains. The tops of which peaked through the turbulent clouds in the same way his thoughts did. Churning within him, *We are wasting valuable time doing*

129

this. If he had known why not send me weeks ago! Why wait until the battle is just about to begin. We are their greatest asset and they send us off on this fool's errand.

Akronius? Syphra interrupted his inner tantrum.

Yes?

Do you know what they say about pride? She asked softly.

Huh? What are you talking abooooouutt, AARRRGGHHHH!!" Akronius screamed as he fell from Syphra's back when she rolled midair.

Syphra! Catch me! Catch Me! HELP! Akronius pled as he plummeted through the air. The freezing wind and snow whipped · across his face, causing him to roll and tumble around and around.

NO! Shift and save yourself since you are so talented. Surely the great Akronius can do something so simple. She responded, flying just out of his reach, circling him like a corkscrew through the sky.

Humbled by her rebuke he focused on their bond and let the magic ripple over his skin, feeling the scales spread down his back, face morphing and elongating. His hands formed large gray claws and wings ripped from his back catching the wind and halting his descent.

Forgive my pride Syphra. Akronius said drifting near her.

Always she replied, *Catch me if you can!* Syphra snapped her wings closed in a dive that sent wind pushing him into a tumble. He did his best to copy her movements as they raced through the air but tired quickly.

Syphra, I can hold this form no longer, he called.

Come closer, I will catch you this time. He heard the smile in her voice and chuckled as he let go of the magic holding him in dragon form, exhausted he landed easily on her broad back, clutching the reins of the saddle that enabled him to ride her.

"It is a good thing I cut holes in my shirts during practice," he said with a chuckle. "Now hurry Syphra, we have a rock to cleanse." They streaked through the boiling clouds towards the mountains.

A scowl sat etched on Ashrek's face as he rode at the front of his army as they passed through the city streets, no cheers echoed in the early dawn, no cries or prayers for their safety. Only the disinterested stares and empty eyes of a conquered and defeated people followed their progress.

"General," Ashek called to the woman at his right.

"Yes, my lord," Lenara answered.

"Have the men aligned three abreast, we will be using the mountain pass to enter Elhaanai undetected."

"As you wish." Slowing her horse she passed the word down the ranks watching as the men shifted into the new position. No one spoke, only the clip-clop of horses' hooves and the clang of metal swords on shields echoed into the winter sky. In the distance stormy gray clouds hovered over the Mnara Mountains, heralding days of violence ahead.

The sun rose higher in the sky as the two armies faced each other yet again in the middle of a nearby field for the fourth day. Kaison could see the children running through the stalks of wheat in his memory, visions of years long past. The field now lay barren beneath the stormy sky, snow falling and piling around them.

Alric stood with the generals watching and waiting, wondering if they should send an emissary; make a last attempt at peace in order to avoid bloodshed. The decision was taken from him as a solitary rider emerged from the ranks and headed their way, they held their breath until the messenger stood before them.

Lowering her hood a beautiful woman sat confidently before them astride a dark horse, "Shama." She nodded towards the white haired oracle before meeting the eyes of each of the others, "And you must be Alric. So young to be so set on an early death. My lord offers you a chance to turn from your misguided beliefs and join him. Everyone who does so will be spared."

"And you are?" Elainea asked.

"Forgive my rudeness, I am Priestess Sybella."

"Witch you mean." Lorenz muttered, grunting as Keuri's elbow struck his ribs.

"Call me whatever you like. Regardless of what you think, I am on the right side of this war. You would be wise to stay in my good graces." Sybella said, narrowing her eyes at the ill-mannered man.

"Sybella, there is still time to turn from this path." Shama said, stepping to the horse's side, "Time to save the lives of all those here, on both sides. Nothing can be found in darkness, only with light can you truly see what lies before you"

"Fool." Sybella shoved him away with her foot. "Tomorrow you will *see* true power. However, my lord is not without mercy, he gives you this last night to lay out your mourning clothes, tomorrow you die."

The dark horse pranced beneath its rider before they both galloped away, disappearing into the ranks of darkness across the field.

Chapter 19

THE SUN WAS JUST BEGINNING TO PEEK over the horizon as Jacob stood outside of the tent holding baby Renee. Lorox was at his side, watching the army head to the field. His gentle voice silently hummed along with those marching to war, he did not know the words but he felt it reverberating down into his bones.

"What are they singing, Lorox?" He asked.

"They are singing to The One, asking for guidance and protection. Thanking him for victory and asking to be allowed into his kingdom should they fall on the field today. They ask to die with honor." Lorox responded solemnly.

"Do you...do you think...can they win?" Jacob's voice trembled slightly as he asked.

"Everything will happen according to the will of The One. We only need to trust, obey and watch it happen. Do our part when it is required and accept the outcome, whatever it may be." Lorox told him.

Jacob nodded and together they watched the shadow of the last soldier disappear over the rise.

Elainea knelt at the edge of the battlefield with Alric on her right and Kaison to her left, Shama stood before them with his arms lifted and eyes closed. She could hear the creaking of armor and the clank of swords as the arm knelt behind them. "Oh mighty and powerful Adi, we humbly come before you this day and ask... no, we beg for your strength and protection. Cause our feet to be sure and our aim true. Do not let us falter in the face of fear. Do not let us be overcome by the enemy. Carry us this day as we carry your light within us, go before us, stay by our side and guard those we leave behind. IWE HIVYO. Let it be so!"

"IWE HIVYO! Let it be so!" the army shouted in response as they rose to their feet, hearts pounding and eyes clear.

"Look at them, kneeling in the snow like children. Praying as if someone is actually listening. It is time we put an end to this charade my Lord. Sound the attack." Sybella said with disgust.

"Someone is always listening, child. Our job is only to stop them from hearing the response." David said.

Sybella looked at him in question but he did not say another word, only lifted his hand and signaled the army forward, his eyes locked onto Alric in the distance.

A war cry shattered the silence as the two sides rushed towards each other, a sound like thunder echoed across the valley as they collided. Sparks flew as iron clashed with iron, shield pushed against shield and the ground turned into a quagmire of blood, mud and snow. The screams of the dying and wounded soon joined the cacophony of battle, regardless of which side they fell, the pain was the same. And across the distance Alric engaged David in a battle of a different nature; they fought on an alternate plane entirely. Their spirit and minds were locked in a match as old as time itself, wrestling for control, darkness and light flashed through the air amid the grunts and growls of wolves and warriors.

Not an hour into battle a trumpet blast was heard from the east, Elainea shoved her sword into the belly of an attacker and spared a glance over her shoulder.

"NO." Her eyes widened as a blood red crest rose over the distant hill, Ashrek was attacking them from behind!

"Argh!" she screamed, as a sword sunk deeply into her left arm. She released a blast of fire that reduced the brave man to ashes at her feet in retaliation.

"Keuri!" she screamed. "We've got a problem!" Gesturing with her chin, to the approaching group of soldiers. Though small in number, it would be taxing to further divide their forces to face this new enemy.

Keuri followed Elainea's line of sight and ground her teeth in determination as she looked around quickly for her brother. Sending a small gust of wind, she knocked the opponent Lorenz was fighting onto his back allowing Lorenz to drive his spear through the man's chest. "Lorenz, send some of the men to the rear!" Keuri shouted, watching as he turned and quickly assessed the situation. Shifting directions he called a few men and Eret to his side as they raced off to face the approaching threat. She whispered a quick plea for his protection as she ducked under the blade of yet another black cloaked attacker.

Ashrek watched Sybella stand at the right hand of the mad King David, seeing her smooth waistline caused his blood to run hotter and rage blinded him. Screaming with fury he drove his sword through the breastplate and out the back of the man who faced him as he tried in vain to hack his way towards where they stood. He imagined he could see the malicious glint in the witch's eye as she watched him get slashed from all sides until one large frame blocked his view entirely. He snarled as he locked eyes with a stocky red haired man who flicked his wrist and sent a man sized boulder hurtling towards him. *At last, a challenger!* Ashrek thought as he shattered the rock into thousands of little pieces, pelting the men around him with its shards. He saw the man's eyes widen with shock and then narrow as they squared off. Ashrek focused on the man, planning to crush him like he had done to so many already on the battlefield and found he was unable to do so. The man's blood seemed too thin, the minerals were in such small amounts that drawing them together did little more than cause an irritating smirk on the man's face.

"Ha ha ha! Sorry boy, that trick won't work with me! Others far stronger than you have tried," Eret taunted, deflecting the boulder

Ashrek flung at his face. The two men flung stones and dirt, created huge gaping holes in the earth and tried to bury each other and anyone who crossed their path in its depths. When they had nearly exhausted themselves they drew swords and clashed viciously. The ringing of their blades melted into the cacophony of the battle that raged around them. Eret blocked a blow with his sword and his free hand grabbed the wrist of Ashrek that held a small dagger.

"Dirty cheat!" He ground out between clenched teeth.

"I. Will. Kill. YOU!" Ashrek grunted as the men continued to strain for the upper hand.

Eret took a step back, landing in a small crevice that wrenched his ankle painfully creating a moment of distraction. Ashrek gleefully slipped the small dagger into the space beside the chest-guard and watched the pain flash across Eret's face. Crying out, Eret wrapped his arms around his enemy, drawing them into a deadly embrace. "For the light," he whispered and directed his waning strength into widening the crevice he had stepped into. Seeing what was happening Ashrek tried to free himself from the other man's grip, screaming in anger as they both fell into the chasm. Though the scream was abruptly silenced no one noticed among the carnage that still raged in every direction. Bodies of ally and enemy lay strewn across the battle torn field. Ashrek had fought viciously draining the strength from scores of men and women before finding his match in Eret.

And still David stood, fists clenched at his side facing Alric across the sea of clashing bodies. Veins pulsing with dark magic he concentrated on the boy who should have been killed before birth and many times since, the boy who claimed no desire for the throne, but who did everything he could to wrest it from his control.

The sweat dripping down Alric's face mixed with the tears flowing from his eyes; so many lost in a battle that could have been avoided. His cousin was possessed and the dark entity refused to back down, refused to accept defeat. The darkness would rather lose every life it had claimed to death rather than concede to the light. Alric grieved for them, for those who fought against him and those who fought by his side, death had taken so many of them. He could feel each soul flicker like candle light, blinking out of existence as if he had blown against the wick himself. But he could not stop. He would fight and push back against the darkness until his last breath if necessary. He fought for those who could not or would not fight for themselves. He fought for children like Jacob and his baby sister, for every child that would be born in the years to come. He fought for his own sister, he could feel her weakening and pushed as much of his strength through the bond as he could spare, praying she could hold on just a little bit longer.

Chapter 20

THEY FOUGHT ON THE CHARRED GROUND on what had been the town surrounding Nuru Manor that David had burned to the ground along with the poor souls who had not managed to escape. It broke Kaison's heart when he first saw it, the blackened skeletal remains of homes that had been filled with life and love. Darkness was an invasive parasite that destroyed everything it came in contact with, it had to be rooted out from the source. Closing his eyes, he breathed deeply and focused on the darkness before him. He could feel the reassuring strength of Shama who stood just behind him, chanting softly in a language known only to him, hoping against hope that Akronius would return in time.

KAISON! DUCK! Naia leapt over the man's head latching onto the throat of an enemy who was approaching his back. Kaison grunted in thanks and fought on with the man before him, finally able to deliver a killing blow. Looking around at the carnage was disheartening; several of the Dire Wolves had given their lives for the cause as had many southerners. Regardless of which side you fought on, blood ran the same red color. He turned at the sound of a warning growl, meeting sword with sword of yet another attacker.

Keuri and Elainea fought side by side, creating a swirling pillar of wind and fire that swept through the men surrounding them. Auni dived in and out amongst the enemy using his great talons to leave poisonous gouges and scratches in his wake, the venom moving swiftly through each victim. First, limbs stopped responding, and then breathing became difficult and eventually impossible as each man died completely aware and in agony.

"I can't keep this up much longer!" Keuri shouted against the angry roar of the enemies.

"Neither can I." Elainea responded, dropping her arms in exhaustion. The battle had been raging for several hours. Both women had given almost everything they had. Elainea's fiery hair hung limp and wet down her back, soaked with sweat and moisture from the snow that was falling in thick clumps. Keuri turned and placed her back against Elainea's, both drawing their swords as the men around them began to advance. Elainea spared a glance in her brother's direction and smiled as she felt him push a small amount of energy her way, just enough to light her sword with flame, causing the men to pause in their advance.

"Come on then! Or are you frightened of two small women." Keuri taunted their attackers, causing them to renew their approach. Both women let loose a battle cry as their clashing swords rang out adding notes to Auni's beautiful and deadly war cry.

Akronius and Syphra battled against the snowstorm as they struggled to make their way back to their friends. The now purified stone was securely wrapped in cloth and lay in his satchel. The trip had taken longer than expected and Akronius had felt on more than one occasion that the storm was not natural in origin. Finally they broke free of the raging wind and the scene below them stirred their blood. From such heights it was impossible to determine who was who, only four figures stood out from the crowd. At one side David stood with Sybella, while Alric stood with Shama at the other, both parties in their own protective shields, which did not permit physical weapons to penetrate but the spiritual warfare was almost visible as it pulsed across the field, casting shadows and then light.

Syphra screamed her rage into the midday sky, causing every hand to pause as they looked up in fear. She tore across the field closest to David, spewing acid on all who stood to guard him. Shifting directions, her massive wings knocked men and women aside, raking across the field like a farmer cutting wheat as she flew low to the ground. Akronius understood and felt her rage. He hoped their own people had possessed the sense to duck. Landing a short distance behind Alric, Akronius dismounted and waited for entrance into the shield, it would only be down long enough for him to toss the stone to Shama. Alric turned his head a fraction and nodded, Akronius tossed the stone and as it flew through the air motion to his left caught his gaze.

"NOOOO!" He screamed, but it was too late. An archer, hidden in nearby shrubbery hoping for just an opening, took his shot. Akronius watched helpless as the arrow flew straight into the chest of Shama. It was as if he felt the blow himself, time seemed to slow down as the oracle simply stood there. Alric faltered, feeling the dip in support, dropped the shield entirely and turned to his mentor in horror.

"No! Shama, no! I need you!" Wrapping his arms around the man he lowered him slowly onto his back. Shama spoke one word, "aisa" a light flashed across the field and every person was frozen in time, motionless.

"Alric, I will not be able to hold this long. Take the stone and place it in the staff. You no longer need me. I told you I would not see you through to the end, but I would be with you as those who came before have been with me. You are chosen, you have been strong and courageous, you have stayed the course set before you by The One. We are proud of you, let me go and take your place. Step into your purpose." Shama pressed the ancient staff into Alric's trembling hands, "Take it."

Alric took the staff and the stone from where it had fallen, placing it within the twisted roots at the top of the staff. It slid into place and began to pulse, vibrating down the staff and into his hand, up his arm and deep into his chest until it matched the beating of his heart. When the two beat as one something clicked within him, causing him to gasp with the force of it.

"It is done." Shama said as he exhaled, slowly his body began to glow, then he faded from view, the blood stained arrow falling to the ground. Golden particles rose and swirled around Alric who still knelt on the ground, a few landing on his face while the rest floated up into the stormy sky. Akronius watched transfixed as Alric stood, his face and eyes glowing so brightly he had to shield his eyes. Turning back to the battlefield Alric released the people from the spell and watched as they resumed the fight, even David had been under the spell though his mind had remained alert to what had transpired, whispering insidiously across the distance.

Give up now boy. The oracle is dead and without him you do not stand a chance against me. The voice of the Dark Lord said.

Shama was my friend but he was only a conduit for the true power. I will not yield the fight when I am on the winning side. This is your last chance, free David from your control and surrender to the light. I will not offer again. Alric responded.

Nothing more was said, Alric watched as David began walking forward, Sybella trailing just behind as bodies dropped around him with every step. Alric looked on in horror as he realized what was happening. David was draining the life from his own men, gathering power for a final strike. This could not be allowed to continue, "Akronius, signal a retreat."

"Retreat? You can't be serious, Alric!" Akronius said.

"Trust me." Alric responded softly.

Leaping onto Syphra's back they took to the skies and signaled the retreat, watching in confusion as those on the ground began to rally to Elainea, steadily backing toward Alric's position. Of the thousands that had come to the fight, only a few hundred remained on either side. Elainea stood on a raised patch of ground in the center of their army while David's remaining forces gathered and began circling like vultures around carrion. Alric had a brief flashback to his first vision, the armored person standing atop the hill surrounded by rival banners and smiled, life was funny he thought. She wore no metal armor, but she was the leader they needed.

Sybella watched with pride as her master decimated everyone in his path, soon this fight would be over and she could retake her place at Damu Manor in Arcana. If he had not already died on this field she would find Ashrek and see to it that he suffered slowly. Stepping over and around bodies that lay like discarded corn husks they made their way closer to the boy who would be king.

Kaison and Naia stood at the edge of the group of soldiers watching David and his witch approach. Kaison had lost track of Devona in the fray and was torn in how he hoped to find her. That changed, as he suddenly saw her come out from the shadows, and approach the pair with outstretched arms. Naia growled, *Traitor.*

Chapter 21

"MY KING," DEVONA SAID, and prostrated herself before the one who inhabited the body of her son. She had learned much in her time with the followers of The One, none of which had changed her mind and desire for revenge.

"Well, well, well. I did not expect you to still be alive after all this time, Devona." David said with a smirk.

"I am nothing if not resilient my lord. I want to apologize for doubting your right to rule, and offer information as a sign of my loyalty." Devona spoke without sparing a glance towards the woman at his side.

"What could you possibly offer us that would be of any use?" Sybella sneered.

"You have been operating under the impression that Alric is trying to usurp the throne but he is not. The prophecy we knew was incomplete, the last line had been lost until now." Devona said, a gleam starting in her eye.

"Oh?" David said curiously, "Enlighten us."

"When the dead King returns, darkness will follow. Evil will fill places left hollow. One throne, one life, one death to claim, one to alter, one to change. The One to judge the two between, no pawn, no rook, no bishop nor king." Devona said.

It took them just as long as it had when she first heard it spoken and she watched as Sybella's eyes tracked from Alric to Elainea and widened. "It can't be!"

"It is, see how they surround her. Alric is destined to take Shama's place after he places her on your throne." Devona watched with unveiled joy as the look of shock faded to anger on their faces. Stepping closer to David she gushed, "Elainea is weak, you will have no problem taking her out. And once she is removed, Alric will crumble in his grief."

"This is valuable information, consider yourself forgiven." David smirked and refocused his attention on Elainea.

"Thank you my lord." Devona bowed her head as David walked past her without another glance, taking the moment of distraction Devona drew a small dagger from her sleeve and slid it into her son's side.

"TRAITOR!" Sybella screamed and lunged at the other woman as David wrenched the bloody knife from his body, glaring at the woman locked in a hold by Sybella's magic.

"I will deal with you later if you survive." He muttered.

"She will not." Sybella said wickedly.

"Do whatever you want with her, I have a would-be queen to kill." David stalked forward once again, dark blood leaking down his side with only a slight hitch in his step.

Kaison loathed his sister, but could not allow her to be killed at the hands of Sybella.. He skirted the battle and made his way to where the two women struggled just in time to see a blade of dark magic appear in Sybella's hand before it was plunged into his sister's stomach. His eyes filled with bitter tears as he watched her fall, Sybella leaving her to die slowly as she rushed to catch up with her master.

Alric saw the moment Sybella and David were told the truth of the prophecy by his aunt, he felt the betrayal deeply. She had seemed to enjoy training Elainea in the ways of royalty, learning how The One loved them. How could she betray them like this! Closing his eyes he tried to dampen the pain, force it into a place to deal with at a later time. Focusing on the steady beat of his heart and the pulse of the staff he clasped it in two hands, lifting it into the air. Then he brought it down quickly, CRACK, it struck the ground and sent a wave of light over the field before him.

"Kneel!" He shouted as he struck the ground again, his voice echoing across the battle. Those who served the light knelt as one, those who did not saw this as surrender and shouted in triumph. The light from the staff swept through those left standing, a scythe claiming its harvest. The darkness separated from each host like wheat from chaff and the bodies fell, alive but unconscious. David, seeing his power supply diminishing, turned and grabbed Sybella by the throat.

"NO! Master don't..." Sybella's words were choked off as she felt her master draining her life and power. She was powerless to stop it, almost. With the last of her power she screamed in pain and disappeared in a puff of sulfuric smoke, leaving David grasping air. All he could do was chuckle. "I will find you pet," he whispered, kicking the shackled stump of leg that remained where she had stood and turned to face Alric.

Kaison knelt beside his sister as she lay writhing in agony, "Devona, I am sorry."

"Do not weep for me!" Devona spat back, shocking him with the vehemence in her voice, "Do not act like you will mourn my death. You are just like every man, just like our father. Neither of you could see me for who I was meant to be. Neither of you cared enough to even try."

"Devona, that is not true! You know I loved you. Despite even what Alanna saw in you, I held onto hope that you could be redeemed." Kaison pled.

"Lies. You are weak, you have always been weak. You knew the man I married was terrible and you did NOTHING. You knew of the horrors he subjected me to and you did NOTHING. You claim love and yet you do nothing to protect your own sister! You think it was by chance that he vanished! I have always looked after myself, taken care of myself, PROTECTED myself." Tears tracked down Kaison's face as he listened to the bitterness in her voice and heard the truth he had suspected, but never truly knew.

"Devona I…" Kaison started.

"NO! I do not want your empty apologies. My husband was not the first and he will not be the last! You did not even raise that boy and yet he has inherited your weakness. He will die protecting his sister. Just like you!" Devona plunged a sword into the belly of her brother, so focused on his own inner turmoil he had not seen her hands searching for it among the fallen weapons strewn about them.

"Why?" He asked, looking down at the blood flowing from the wound.

"Your birth stole everything from me. Alric's stole everything from my son. And my son stole what little I had grasped for myself. I will make sure the same is done to both our sons, even if I do not live to see it happen, I will destroy everyone and everything they hold dear," Devona said, her breath faltering through the gore bubbling from her lips.

Kaison slumped to the side as a howl pierced through the battle in the distance, Naia. He could see her limping her way to his side; she fell and got up only to fall again with a whimper. The bond between them was breaking, when it was severed completely both would die. *Kaison,* she whispered through their bond. Too weak for anything more, they waited for the end, separated by space but together in heart.

Chapter 22

SYPHRA AND AKRONIUS STILL HOVERED in the air watching the light flash across the field dispelling the darkness. He and Syphra had completed their mission, though initially both had wanted to be in the heat of battle Alric had decided they were best suited to carry the stone. He was right, and for that Akronius was grateful. He had fought many battles and was tired of the blood stains on his soul. Despite the force of Alric's light, David pressed forwards, now making his way toward Elainea. Syphra dropped like a stone without a word being spoken, landing her large frame with David before her and their army behind them.

"You DARE think to stand between me and my prize?" David shouted, "You are nothing! Step aside or die."

Syphra growled and spewed acid at the man standing against them, it completely coated him from head to toe and he simply wiped it away as if it were mud. "As I said, you are nothing." David's dark eyes seemed to grow even wider as he began to chant and stretched his hand out towards them. The waves of light were coming faster now, the pulses closer together and gathering strength. They pushed against David who dug his heels into the snow-covered earth against the onslaught.

Syphra began to groan, clawing at her own head in pain as Akronius screamed and dropped to his knees.

Akronius, you must shift. That is the only way you will survive this. His power is too strong for your human mind to process. SHIFT!

"I. Can't." Akronius ground out through clenched teeth, blood beginning to leak from his ears and nose. Darkness surrounded him as her voice soothed the pain away, *I will help you.*

Having dealt with the arrogant man and his dragon, David once again turned his attention to Elainea. Alric watched Elainea shift her stance and face the approaching danger, he watched Keuri position herself in front of his sister. He watched Akronious and Syphra fall, he watched Kaison fall. He watched Auni struck down by an arrow, he watched the generals fall one by one as they fought to protect his sister, their queen. The prophecy had given direction, but her words the night before had inspired loyalty.

STEP INTO YOUR PURPOSE, the last words of his friend and mentor floated on the breeze and he took a single step forward, and then another and another. With each step he felt power flooding his body. He felt the presence of every oracle that had come before him and the hope of the one who would come after him. With each step his sight sharpened, he could see the dormant gifts in each of the warriors before him and he beckoned them to himself. He touched each spark and drew power until he glowed and overflowed with it. Unlike David who stole the life of his followers, Alric opened himself to the life force around him, allowing it to flow through him and back again like a cycle. Taking a final step he brought the staff down with such force that it drove down into the ground, traveling across the earth like a river of light until it reached the place David stood and grabbed hold of him. It held him rooted to the spot and though he struggled, flung curse after curse towards the people before him, his words could not penetrate the light.

"NO! You will not win! I am destined to rule! You are not powerful enough!" David's angry voice raged against the power as it moved up his body slowly, engulfing him into a cocoon of pure light. Silence stretched across the battlefield as they all processed what had happened, was it possible they had won? Had darkness truly been purged?

Alric let the pulses slow and then fade, as he made his way onto the battlefield, the crowd parting silently for him. Elainea stood there as he approached, coated in blood and weak, her left arm hanging limply at her side thanks to a deep wound. Keuri, who had multiple wounds, leaned heavily on the arm of her brother, both dipped their heads as he passed them and grasped his sister and pulled her into a hug. The trio followed behind him as he went to where Akronius had fallen, the crowd began to murmur in awe. There were two dragons now, one with deep scars across its large gray snout.

"Do you wish to remain like this? I can help you change back," Alric asked, only to have the beast shake its head, its black eyes deep but peaceful. "As you wish. You will have no memory of your human life, your name will be Rako. I only ask that you carry Auni back to the mountain to heal, I will join you there shortly." Alric placed a hand on the creature, smiling sadly as recognition faded from his eyes. Stepping back he watched the two majestic creatures take to the skies, the injured Auni clasped in Rako's claw, and fly off into the distance. Syphra would take care of him, no one was created to be alone.

Alric followed a groove in the earth and found the body of Naia, who had dragged herself to where his father lay barely breathing.

"You've done well, son. I am proud of you." Kaison winced and forced himself to continue, "Your mothers would have been proud. They are proud."

"Father, we have healers. I can bring one of them to you." Alric offered though he knew the answer.

"No, Alric. I have been apart from Alanna long enough. Let me go. I… I love you son." Kaison whispered as his strength faded, "Naia...please. Naia."

Alric watched his father struggle to hold on to the last flicker of life, "I will release her from the bond. She will live." Alric said as he passed a hand through the Dire wolf's fur. Kaison relaxed as he saw her chest rise and fall with a full breath.

"Thank you," he whispered and exhaled, smiling at something no one else could see.

Alric bowed his head and finally let the tears flow, so much had been lost. Taking a few moments to compose himself he turned to address those who remained. Slowly, those who had been freed from the hold of darkness began to rouse and stand. Among them a group of fierce dark skinned women made their way to the front, and knelt before Alric.

"I am Lenara, my lord. We are the last of the tribe of Nitralii. Ages ago we numbered in the thousands and were the defenders of the throne. Over time we were blinded and led astray by pride, we five are all that are left. I lost my daughter, Serena, in the battle today. I would ask your forgiveness, once we have journeyed to the mountain and been purified once more, I offer our services and pledge our lives for the light."

"Rise Lenara. We have all lost friends and family today, whether you fought for the light or against it. The blood shed here will not have been in vain. We came here as enemies, but we will leave these grounds united." Addressing the crowd he spoke louder, "I will not force you to believe as we do, but I offer you the chance to learn and hopefully one day you will choose on your own. The One does not demand blind obedience out of fear, the choice is and always will be yours. Only you can choose whom you will serve, if you are able to live peacefully with us, please do so. If you are not, there are other cities you may find more hospitable. Whatever you decide, you have my blessing. Many of you who fought on the side of darkness were told I would sit on the throne. That was a lie."

Alric looked around at the mix of men and women as they began to talk amongst themselves. "I will take my place as guardian on the mountain, no more will kings lead you astray. From this day forward, you will bow to another. To Queen Elainea." Alric gestured to his sister who lifted her chin and met the shocked and curious gazes of those around her. Lenara smiled and took her warriors to flank their new Queen.

Alric walked the distance to where David stood encased in light and stood for a moment, staring at the swirling darkness behind the light as it struggled in vain to escape. Every now and then there was a break in mass and the tortured face of his cousin was visible. Placing the tip of his staff against the casing Alric watched as the light receded from the ground traveling up over David's body. When at last David was free, an orb of viscous darkness floated above his head as he swayed and collapsed. Though still a young man in years, David's frame was emaciated and gaunt, his skin stretched across bones like wax paper, his hair brittle and sparse across a mottled scalp.

"Have our healers tend to him," Alric said. "He is just as much a victim of the darkness as any of us."

Alric pointed the staff at the dark orb and lowered it down into one of the chasms Eret had created during the battle. Once it was as far down as he could take it, he instructed one of the others able to move earth to cover it and close the fissure.

"Is it finished?" Elainea whispered.

"It will never be finished, until The One says it is." Alric took his sister's hand. "Darkness is as much a part of light as the day is a part of night. You cannot appreciate one without the other. But, the battle is over for now."

"Will the Dark Lord return?" a soldier shouted from the crowd.

Alric turned and looked over the battle worn group. "The Dark Lord will always try to return. He only needs an ear who will listen and a willing heart to do his bidding. Guard your hearts above all else. Stay alert, stay ready. If the need for battle comes again, you will know."

Slowly the group dispersed to gather and bury the dead, the time for mourning had come.

"What will you do now, Alric?" Elainea asked. Fear and uncertainty laced her words.

"I will see you placed on the throne and then head to the mountain and take my place." Alric said looking at his sister, "I will visit often. You know I can't cook, Laney."

Elainea laughed and hugged Alric with her good arm.

"Come on, let's see to your people," he said.

"OUR people Alric, they are OUR people now," she replied as they walked back towards the people together.

Epilogue

THE DAY DAWNED CLEAR, the streets and market were once again bustling with life. Vendors haggling over prices and children chasing each other as laughter filled the air. Jacob, with Renee strapped to his back, scurried from the kitchen as the cook flapped a towel at them, stopping him from sneaking more of the pastries meant for the queen's table. The toddler's laughter was like silver bells that bounced around the warm room in their wake.

"Are you ready?" Alric asked his sister.

"No. Are you?" She responded quickly. Keuri had finished braiding her hair into an intricate pattern that would support the crown once it was placed on her head. The siblings had unanimously decided to destroy the crown worn by David and had a new one crafted by talented metal workers under Alric's guidance. He had it fashioned to resemble the intricate roots of the great tree in the glade where he had met The One. Only he knew of its hidden meaning, to onlookers it was simply a beautiful design with precious gems sprinkled here and there.

"We are as ready as we'll ever be sis. Let's go. The sooner we do this, the sooner we can eat!" Alric said with a wink as he offered his arm.

"Of course you're thinking of food." Elainea slipped her right arm into his and walked down the hall of Nuru Manor. They were brightly lit from the open windows, the manor and surrounding town had been reconstructed in the months since the dark battle. Everything was new and open and filled with life and light. The secret passageways had been filled and closed, the dungeons destroyed along with all of Chumbra's things. As the siblings entered the great hall they stopped at two pillars holding up the arched ceiling. At the top on the right Kaison Bearclaw was inscribed and on the other Allanna Bearclaw and Wleia Mwandishi, below them each name of those who sacrificed their life was etched. They were the pillars on which the future would be built, they would not be forgotten.

A trumpet sounded. "Presenting her royal highness, Queen Elainea Mwandishi, and the Oracle, Alric Bearclaw Mwandishi!"

Thunderous applause greeted them as they made their way to the front of the room.

Elainea stood before the crowd and received her crown. "We have fought hard to be where we are now. Some sacrificed a little; many gave their all to see that we succeeded. We have lost brothers and sisters, mothers and fathers, wives and husbands, sons and daughters. They will not be forgotten. Together we can create a future that will honor them. Together we can make the future safe for generations to come. Together we can follow The One into our destiny!" Raising her fist into the air to the applause, the empty left sleeve folded against her side fluttered slightly in the breeze. Inhaling the sweet fragrance of candied dates, she smiled and glanced to where Alric had been standing only to find him gone.

"Show off," she muttered, turning back to the people before her with a wide smile.

THE END

Acknowledgments

It's here!   I did it and I am so proud of myself and grateful to everyone for cheering me along on this journey. To my parents who celebrated every milestone, my daughter who thinks mommy is cool now, and my husband who encouraged me to keep writing, just keep writing.

To the readers who have left reviews and to my writing community that daily challenged and inspired me. This tale may be at the end, but there is so much more to come.

COME! Follow me! Let's go on another adventure!

www.nicolepatricethomas.com

www.ingramcontent.com/pod-product-compliance
Lightning Source LLC
Chambersburg PA
CBHW070656100726
47907CB00007B/2227